Also by Greg van Eekhout

Voyage of the Dogs

GREG VAN EEKHOUT

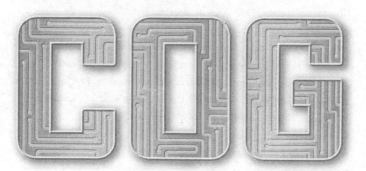

HARPER

An Imprint of HarperCollins*Publishers*

Library of Congress Cataloging-in-Publication Data

Names: Van Eekhout, Greg.

Title: Cog / Greg van Eekhout ; illustrated by Beatrice Blue.

Description: New York, NY : Harper, an imprint of HarperCollins
    Publishers, [2019] | Summary: "After an accident leaves him
    damaged and separated from his scientist caregiver, a young
    android recruits four robot accomplices and embarks on a cross-
    country road trip to reunite with her"—Provided by publisher.

Identifiers: LCCN 2019009522 | ISBN 978-0-06-268607-7 (hardback) |
    ISBN 978-0-06-295835-8 (special edition)

Subjects: | CYAC: Robots--Fiction. | Science fiction. | BISAC:
    JUVENILE FICTION / Animals / Dogs. | JUVENILE FICTION
    / Science Fiction. | JUVENILE FICTION / Action & Adventure
    / Survival Stories.

Classification: LCC PZ7.V2744 Cog 2019 | DDC [Fic]--dc23 LC
    record available at https://lccn.loc.gov/2019009522

Typography by Molly Fehr

19 20 21 22 23   PC/LSCH   10 9 8 7 6 5 4 3 2 1

❖

First Edition

To Deb Coates, Sarah Prineas, and Jenn Reese, for years of good conversation, shared meals, and cognitive development.

✳ ✳ ✳

CHAPTER 1

MY NAME IS COG. Cog is short for "cognitive development." Cognitive development is the process of learning how to think and understand.

In appearance, I am a twelve-year-old boy of average height and weight. This means I'm fifty-eight inches tall and weigh about ninety pounds and seven ounces. In actuality, I am seven months old.

Now I will tell you some facts I have learned about platypuses.

Platypuses are carnivorous mammals with thick fur like otters and paddle-shaped tails like beavers and bills and webbed feet like ducks.

Male platypuses have a sharp spur on their hind feet that delivers venom.

Platypuses have no stomachs.

The story I am about to tell you has nothing to do with platypuses. But when I learn something, I enjoy telling people about it. It is part of my programming. I have learned many things about platypuses. I have learned many things about many things. My life is a story about learning things. I am happy to have learned some things and unhappy to have learned other things.

This story is me, Cog, telling you about all the things.

I live in a room with a bed where I lie down. It is called a bedroom. I have shelves for my 1,749 books on topics including mummies and rockets and marsupials and knights. Reading is one of the ways in which I increase my cognitive development. Sometimes, when I am supposed to be in sleep mode, I lie in my bed, reading my books, looking at the glowing stars stuck to my ceiling and imagining I am under the real night sky.

I am not good at sleeping. It is a bug.

After my bedroom, my favorite room in the house is the

kitchen. This is where biofuel is stored and prepared. Pizza is my favorite biofuel. There are cupboards for dishes and cups and drawers for forks and spoons and knives. There is a machine in the kitchen for washing these items. The dishwashing machine just washes dishes. It is not good at conversation.

Another room in the house is the living room. It contains a large television and squishy furniture. Sitting on squishy furniture and watching television is defined as "living."

The largest room in the house is the laboratory. It is equipped with tool chests, computers, and a 3D fabricator. There is a table upon which I often lie while Gina Cohen makes repairs and adjustments to me.

Gina is a scientist for uniMIND. She has brown eyes like my visual sensors and brown skin like my synthetic dermal layer. Her hair is black and shiny, like the feathers of birds in the corvid family, which includes crows and ravens. When she smiles, which is often, a small gap is evident between her two front teeth. My teeth, which are oral mastication plates, have no gap, but I enjoy practicing smiling with Gina.

✳ ✳ ✳

I spend most days engaged in educational activities. Sometimes this means solving puzzles. Sometimes it means practicing simple tasks, like tying my shoes, or preparing my own biofuel in the kitchen. Sometimes it means sitting on the lab table while Gina opens my skull and does things with screwdrivers to my brain.

And sometimes, but not very often, I engage in learning outside the house.

This morning Gina takes me outside.

We drive down the curving streets that lead away from home. My olfactory sensors detect the spice of pine trees and the sweet scent of grass. Birds chirp and flit among trees.

"Nice to be outside, huh?" Gina says, showing the space in her teeth.

The sky is bright blue. Somewhere out there, unseen in daylight, real stars shine. I am with my friend, and I am going to learn.

"It is very nice," I agree.

Today's lesson is shopping. Shopping is the process by which products are obtained, and this process is conducted in a building called a "shop" or a "store" or, as is the case today, a "Giganto Food Super Mart."

Gina parks the van and shows me where to get a shopping cart. It takes three tries before we find one that doesn't have a stuck or wobbly wheel.

"These carts have bugs," I report.

Gina laughs and says, "Yes, Cog. It seems most shopping carts do."

Bugs are mistakes. I have quite a few, but Gina tells me not to worry about them, because most things are buggy. Gina works to eliminate my bugs all the time.

We go over a rubber mat, and the glass doors of Giganto Food Super Mart slide open. I think I experience a bug now, because for a moment I just stand in the entrance, overwhelmed. Giganto Food Super Mart is a single room that is wider and taller and goes back farther than any room I have ever experienced before. Lights blaze from the ceilings. Music plays from somewhere I cannot see. People wind through aisles with buggy shopping carts filled with biofuel.

Gina brings me back to attention by handing me a list. There are thirty-four items, and it covers two sides of a sheet of paper.

"These are all the things we need, Cog. The items are

located in different parts of the store." She points out signs hung above each aisle. "The signs will show you where some of the items are located. But some items aren't marked on the signs, so you'll have to devise other ways of locating them."

"Are you not going to be supervising me?"

"Nope! Remember, the point of this lesson isn't just shopping. It's learning how to be independent."

"I assumed you would be walking alongside me as I was learning to be independent."

She waves her hand toward a cluster of chairs and tables on the far side of the store. "I'll be right over there, drinking coffee and catching up on work." She ruffles my hair. "You can do this."

I take a look at my list and begin pushing my cart.

Cheese is the first item. Moving along the end of the aisles and reading the signs, I find the cheese aisle quite independently. The cheese is kept in an open refrigerated case. There are racks and racks of cheese. Bins of cheese. Round blocks of cheese. Rectangular blocks of cheese. Square packs of sliced cheese. Bags of shredded cheese hanging from hooks. American cheese. Mexican cheese. Italian cheese. Monterey Jack cheese. Pepper Jack cheese. Mozzarella cheese. Cheddar cheese. Sharp cheddar cheese. Mild cheddar cheese. Romano cheese. Parmesan cheese. Shredded Mexican cheese blend. Shredded Italian cheese blend. Cream cheese. String cheese. Goat cheese. Whizzy Cheese, which is a kind of cheese that sprays forth from a can.

When I walked into Giganto Food Super Mart I possessed a vocabulary of 37,432 words. In the time I have stood in the cheese aisle, my vocabulary has increased by fourteen. All my new vocabulary involves cheese.

I load the cart with every kind of cheese, including four blocks of mozzarella cheese, because mozzarella cheese is pizza cheese. The cart is full when I finally push it away from the cheese aisle. The wheel wobbles. I suppose bugs can arise at any moment.

The next item on my list is toothpaste, and I find the toothpaste very independently.

There are almost as many varieties of toothpaste as cheese.

But maybe I do not need to obtain toothpaste. Toothpaste and Whizzy Cheese seem to share key similarities. Perhaps I can brush my teeth with Whizzy Cheese.

I skip toothpaste and continue to the next item on my list.

✳ ✳ ✳

I am not very good at shopping, it turns out.

I report back to Gina, struggling along with two buggy shopping carts piled with mounds of cheese and toilet paper and peanut butter and no toothpaste. She puts her hand on her forehead, a gesture that I have learned can mean she has a headache.

"You did not put aspirin on the list, but I know where it is. I will go get another cart."

"No, no, thank you, Cog. I'm fine. It's just . . ." She takes out her notebook and clicks open her pen. "Can you tell me how you made your shopping decisions?"

I explain my cheese dilemma to her and my idea about brushing my teeth with Whizzy Cheese. She nods a lot and jots down notes.

When she is done taking notes, she clicks her pen closed and pockets her notebook. "Well, we have some things to work on, mainly concerned with judgment. But for a first attempt, you did a very good job, Cog."

I feel warm inside. It is a familiar sensation, something I experience whenever Gina tells me I have done something well.

"But we actually don't need all this cheese," she continues. "Nor do we need seven dozen apples or eight different kinds of orange juice or twelve different varieties of dish soap. So let's start putting most of this back."

I learn that unshopping takes longer than shopping.

As we return items to shelves, Gina explains to me where my judgment was faulty and led me astray.

"Is my judgment the result of a bug?" I ask her. "Can you fix it?"

"No," she says, hanging seven bags of shredded cheese back on their hooks. "It's just something you have to learn. It's like my old professor used to tell me: 'Good judgment comes from experience, but experience comes from bad judgment.' That means we learn by making mistakes."

I process this for a while.

"How long did it take you to learn good judgment?"

"Oh, I'm still learning it, buddy. I'm learning it all the time."

That night as I lie in my room, unable to enter sleep mode, I look at my stars. I imagine I can see beyond them, through the ceiling of my room, through the roof, through the sky.

I think about what Gina told me.

We learn by making mistakes.

I am Cog. Short for "cognitive development." I am built to learn. Which must mean I am built to make mistakes.

I form a decision: To increase my learning, tomorrow I shall make some big mistakes.

CHAPTER 2

WHEN MORNING COMES I CONSUME my portion of biofuel, which is called breakfast.

I am supposed to clean myself and get dressed before joining Gina in the laboratory for my learning period, but instead of going to the lab, I walk very quietly down the hall and cross the living room to the front door.

The door is kept locked and requires a key, but only from the outside. I am not certain, but I believe this is meant to protect our property. Property is what belongs to you.

Leaving the house without Gina's permission is a mistake. This pleases me, because a mistake is an act of bad judgment, and I expect my act of bad judgment to increase my cognitive development.

I step out into the world.

Today the world is gray, with a cold breeze that chills my syntha-derm skin.

I have already made another mistake: I should have worn a jacket.

I am pleased at having gained the experience of regret.

The skies darken and the wind picks up. A drop of water plunks against my cheek. Another drop strikes my face, and then drops fall everywhere. They batter the leaves in the trees. Deep puddles form on the sidewalk. A river flows next to the curb, carrying dead leaves and twigs and candy wrappers. Raindrops splatter off rooftops and darken the pavement. Rain soaks through my clothes. Water seeps through my canvas sneakers, and my socks squelch like sponges with every step.

This is not the first time I have experienced plunking water, but the previous times were all inside, in the shower, which is a water-spraying device used for cleaning purposes.

My circulation pump quickens in my chest. I am learning.

I hear the truck before I see it, an engine roar that tells

me something big is coming. It squeals around the corner, bright blue with a shiny grill like gnashing mastication plates. Dirty rainwater sprays from its tires.

The driver is not watching the road. Instead, he examines himself in his rearview mirror, a finger embedded deep inside his left nostril. I have observed this behavior in other humans and understand that he is attempting to remove desiccated mucus fragments from his nose. These fragments are known as boogers.

As the truck thunders on, a black-and-white Chihuahua trots across the street in its path. Its little paws make tiny splashes in the water.

The Chihuahua sees the truck. It freezes.

The driver does not see the Chihuahua.

I do a word problem:

A pickup truck weighing at least three thousand pounds travels at a rate of forty-five miles per hour toward a four-pound Chihuahua. If a boy is standing on the sidewalk at a distance of twelve feet away, does he have time to save the dog?

I run into the road.

I do not calculate the damage to the boy.

✧ ✧ ✧

My sneakers splash hard on the pavement, wet leaves squishing beneath my feet. Everything around me slows. The chirps of sparrows in the trees draw out to low-pitched moans. The raindrops descend sluggishly to the ground. Maybe my internal clock is buggy.

With a burst of effort, I close the distance and leap in front of the Chihuahua.

What will I learn from this experience? How will this increase my cognitive development?

The truck strikes me and my world goes dark. There is no sound and I am no longer self-aware. Maybe I go offline.

When I become aware once more, the truck is running up the sidewalk, narrowly missing a mailbox. It thumps back down the curb and then continues on as if nothing has happened, leaving rooster tails of sooty rainwater in its wake. The driver never stops. He never gets out of his truck to see if he's harmed anyone. Picking mucus fragments must occupy all his attention.

I lie in the road beside the curb, my body damming up a river of water and cigarette butts. My pain sensors are in the red.

Out in the street lies one of my shoes, scuffed and soaked, with the sock still inside it. My other shoe remains on my foot. I sit on the curb, wet and dirty, and run a full diagnostic check to assess my damage.

My palms and belly are black with road grit. My clothes are torn and filthy. Gently, I run a hand through my sopping hair and feel something that makes the biofuel container inside my belly sink. A bundle of wires pokes through a crack in my skull. I try to tuck the bundle back in and re-arrange my hair to cover the crack, but it is no use.

Covering the wires with my hand, I struggle to my feet. A few cars pass, splashing more muddy water on me, but they do not stop. No one seems to notice me through the rain.

The Chihuahua stands several yards away, dirty but unharmed. With a wag of its tail, it barks at me and turns, trotting down the sidewalk. I watch it duck under a fence and vanish into a yard.

It is home.

I take comfort in this.

But I am badly damaged, and my pain sensors keep putting out strong signals.

Lubrication leaks from my eyes and falls down my cheeks. I have gained more experience than I had anticipated.

I wish the learning would stop now.

CHAPTER 3

STARS SHINE DOWN ON ME when I come back online.

My fingers expect to touch hard, wet asphalt, but instead they feel bedsheets. I am not outside, left alone in the rain after getting hit by the truck. I am in bed, and the stars are the glow-in-the-dark stickers on my ceiling. I must have gone offline again, and then Gina found me and carried me here and tucked me in.

Slowly, I ease myself up and lean back against my pillows. Cables snake from the data ports beneath my flipped-up fingernails to a laptop on my nightstand. I study the readouts but do not understand them. I resolve to ask Gina to explain them to me.

Things are . . . not right. They are not standard.

My right arm is different. Instead of brown syntha-derm, it is white plastic. Perhaps I was so damaged by the truck that it could not be fixed and had to be replaced entirely.

The same is true for my left knee. The right knee is mine, but it is scratched and scuffed. Fortunately I can still bend it, which is the purpose of a knee.

At least there are no wires poking out of my head.

Glancing around the room, I see my posters. I see my models. I see my books. But where the window should be, there is only a plain, white wall. And when I swing my legs over the side of the bed, instead of my bedroom's thick, green carpet, my bare feet touch thin rug.

My things are here. I am here. But this is not my room.

After unplugging the cables from my data ports and flipping my fingernails back down, I take a few steps toward the door.

My left knee feels too loose and my right knee feels stiff and clicks when I try to walk, and I topple face-first into my dresser.

I thought I had already learned balance, but I will have to learn it again.

The doorknob at home is shaped like a ball. This one is shaped like an *L*. Before I can open the door, it opens on me. Standing in the doorway is a trash can with two arms and a boxy head on a telescoping pole, all of it sitting on tank treads.

"Do you have any waste to dispose of?"

I recognize it as a fellow robot.

"Where am I?"

A red light blinks behind a faceplate of black glass.

"Do you have any waste to dispose of?" it asks again.

A man steps behind the robot. "Not right now," he says. "Thank you, Trashbot."

The robot's faceplate blinks green, and it trundles away down the hallway.

The man smiles at me. He does not have a gap between his two front teeth. The frames of his glasses are black, thick plastic. I like them. Glasses are worn by people when their eyes do not function at one hundred percent efficiency. Perhaps I can ask Gina to lower the efficiency of my eyes so that I, too, can wear glasses.

"I am Cog," I say.

"I know. I'm Nathan, and you should be lying down."

He places a hand on my elbow and gently guides me

back toward my bed.

Correction: not my bed. The bed they have supplied in this room that is not my room.

He flips my fingernails back up and reconnects the cables to my data ports.

"How do you feel?" says Nathan.

"I feel like I was hit by a truck and then went offline and then came back online in a place I have never been before."

He examines the readouts on the laptop. "Well, you haven't been in this room, but you've been in this building before. In fact, you started out here. This is uniMIND headquarters."

For a moment I silently process this. "When will I be returning home?"

Nathan displays his gapless smile.

"You're home now, Cog. This is home."

CHAPTER 4

OVER THE NEXT FEW DAYS uniMIND engineers and technicians make more repairs to my damaged body. They cover my new knee with syntha-derm, but my new arm remains white plastic because they have to order brown syntha-derm that matches the rest of me from another uniMIND facility. They also run many tests on my brain. I spend a lot of time with my fingernails flipped up.

When they are not running tests or doing repairs, Nathan shows me around the uniMIND headquarters. Or as he calls it, the campus.

He takes me to a giant central room with a ceiling that soars hundreds of feet above. It is many times bigger than Giganto Food Super Mart. A great redwood tree trunk rises from the floor, disappearing through a hole in the ceiling. It is by far the largest tree I have ever seen. A door in the bark slides open, and Nathan gestures with a sweeping hand. "After you."

"This is a tree," I say. "We are entering a tree."

He laughs. "It's an elevator shaft. I mean, it used to be a redwood, but we had it cut down and hollowed out and converted to an elevator shaft. Pretty cool, huh? It's won a bunch of design awards."

"Where did the tree come from?"

"Don't worry, it's not from a national forest or anything like that. It came off uniMIND property."

I knew one could own a block of cheese. I did not know one could own a tree. Already, I am learning.

The doors slide shut and we go up.

Through windows in the tree, I watch people move along open walkways that ring the vast room, and behind the walkways are glass-walled offices. Some of the rooms are larger, with long tables and groups of people talking and examining charts and graphs projected onto screens.

Nathan looks at me in a way that reminds me of Gina when she is about to teach me something important. "Cog, we're doing very important work here at uniMIND. We're pushing the frontiers of science and technology. And you are a crucial part of that work. We need your help with it. And my job is to make sure you're taken care of. So, don't you worry about a thing. Okay, partner?"

"Okay. I will try not to worry about all the things I am worried about. Okay."

When the elevator stops, we exit the tree and I follow Nathan into another room.

"This is the Biomatonics Lab." Rays of natural sunlight stream in through the windowed ceiling. Vines crawl up the walls, and the air smells of flowers. Birds chirp. Water gurgles over rocks. A butterfly lands on Nathan's shoulder.

"Hold out your hand, Cog."

After a moment of consideration, I do as Nathan says. The butterfly flutters over to my finger.

I have seen butterflies before, darting between the blooms in Gina's backyard. This creature is similar, with twitching antennae and pearly wings of deep purple and yellow. This is all standard. But this butterfly also has little glowing red lights running down its back. This is not standard.

"It is mechanical," I observe.

"You got it. It's a biomaton, a robot modeled after a natural creature."

"Humans are natural creatures," I say.

Nathan nods. "True enough."

"That makes me a biomaton."

He seems surprised. "Well, yeah. Didn't Gina ever tell you that?"

"No."

"What did she call you, then?"

"She called me Cog."

"Let's see some other biomatons, and you can decide for yourself if being a biomaton is a cool thing to be."

He shows me a glass box the size of a refrigerator laid on its side. Inside, a glimmering, jittery mass moves around rocks. When I lean in closer I see that the mass is made up of tiny silver bits, like little crawling pills with legs.

"They look like ants."

Nathan joins me at the box. "That's what they are. Autonomous Nature Technology. ANTs, for short. I came up with that." He laughs and waits for a response, but I do not know what response is standard, so I remain silent. He clears his throat. "'Autonomous' means they function on their own without needing instructions from anyone.

'Nature' is because they mimic creatures from nature. And 'Technology,' because . . . well, technology."

The ANTs swarm across a bridge between two rocks.

"We didn't program them with knowledge of how to build a bridge. We didn't even give them the materials. They figured it all out on their own."

"What did they build it out of?" I ask.

"Look for yourself."

I step closer, putting my nose to the glass. I do not see it at first. It is like one of those smudgy paintings that you have to stare at a long time before you can tell what it is depicting, and I have learned that looking at something a long time is often the only way you ever actually know what you are looking at. So that is what I do.

Finally, I see it. The bridge is made out of the legs of other ANTs.

I watch as three of the ANTs pull the legs off a fourth ANT. When the legs are removed, they push its body over the rock's edge, where it joins a growing pile of other legless ANTs.

"Pretty clever, isn't it?"

"Clever," I say, remembering that I, too, am an autonomous piece of technology based upon another creature. I rub my knee and follow Nathan to another lab. uniMIND workers tap things into tablets and work at computers and say things on phones. They all dress very much like Nathan in light-colored polo shirts.

Here, Nathan shows me a cage housing three mice. They are small and clean and white, with shiny black eyes and pink paws and gleaming silver disks that they wear like hats.

"Are these biomatons as well?" I ask.

"No, they're living creatures, but with a difference. See those disks? They're connected to their brains. Don't worry, it doesn't hurt them."

The mice are very active. They gnaw on wood. They eat seeds. They run on their wheel. These are all standard mouse things.

"What do the disks do?"

Nathan answers by taking his phone out of his pocket. He taps the screen and brings up an interface with the uni-MIND logo and buttons. He presses one of the buttons.

The mice stop gnawing on wood. They stop eating seeds. They stop running on their wheel. He presses another button, and the mice all stand on their hind legs and look at Nathan. He presses a third button. The mice go to their food bowl. Working together, they push it to the center of the cage.

"Pretty cool, huh?"

"You made the mice do that?"

He smiles. "Yep."

"What is the purpose of making mice move a food dish?"

"It's not about the food dish, Cog. It's about the ability to make them do it. Or do anything we want them to."

I do not understand the purpose of making mice do what you want them to. How many things can mice do that are useful?

"Mice are just the beginning," he says. "It's proof of concept. If we can do this with mice, we can do it with other creatures. Dogs. Monkeys. Dolphins. Humans. uniMIND isn't just the name of the company, Cog. It's the name of the technology. The whole aim of everything we do is to develop the uniMIND. Now, I want you to understand that we don't show the uniMIND to everybody. It's very special. Showing it to you means you are very special. Understand?"

I blink, processing.

"No."

He laughs. "You will, Cog. You will."

"When will I see Gina?"

Nathan clears his throat. Perhaps he has a cold.

"Gina doesn't work here anymore, Cog."

"Yes, I know this. Gina does not work at the uniMIND campus. Gina works at home. When will I be going home?"

Nathan smiles, but it is a very different kind of smile. It is a smaller kind that shows no teeth. I am unfamiliar with this kind of smile. It does not convey happiness or excitement or agreeability.

"Cog, this is your home now. Your home is with us, here at the campus. You got damaged at the house with Gina, and we don't want to let that happen again. So, you'll be staying here."

I attempt to regulate the beating of my central circulation pump. "Gina . . . does Gina not wish to be here with me?"

Nathan crouches down so our eyes are on the same level. He puts a hand on my shoulder. "It's not that, Cog. Of course Gina wants to be with you. It's just . . . after you were injured, she was reassigned to another uniMIND location. One far away, where they do . . . other kinds of work. But, listen, buddy, don't worry about her. She's a great engineer. She'll be fine. And believe me, she didn't want to leave you. She's heartbroken."

I ask Nathan to discontinue our tour of my new home and take me back to my room. Though, of course, it is not my room. My room is in the house with Gina.

Gina is damaged.

Her heart is broken.

When one is broken, one must be returned to head-quarters for repair.

One must be taken home.

If Gina's heart is broken, she will attempt to go home.

I will find her there.

CHAPTER 5

I REMAIN BAD AT SLEEPING. Gina said sleep is difficult is for me because my brain is always working, thinking, learning, and she didn't want to "go monkeying around" in my brain before she fully understood what was going on inside my head.

I know about monkeys. Monkeys are nonhuman primate mammals. They are intelligent. But "monkeying around" means to go about things in a way that is not intelligent.

It does not make sense.

Being awake wasn't so bad when I was home. I could lie in my bed and process all the things I learned during the day and look forward to the things I would learn tomorrow. And when I no longer wished to lie awake I could go downstairs and find Gina. Gina is not very good at sleeping, either. Even though she is not a robot, we have some of the same bugs.

On one such night, I prepared two mugs of hot cocoa in the microwave oven, which is a machine that is not capable of learning but is very good at making hot cocoa. Gina was in the laboratory, sitting at her computer. I put her mug on the desk.

Usually she would say "thank you," which is standard behavior. And then I would say "you're welcome" or "no problem" or "think nothing of it," all of which are standard responses. But this time she didn't say anything. She didn't even seem to notice I was there. She just stared at her computer screen with abnormally hydrated eyes. A drop of fluid fell down her cheek.

A face stared out from the screen. Eyes, brown like mine. Nose, a similar shape, narrow in the bridge with a rounded tip. Skin the same shade of brown as my syntha-derm sheath. Hair like mine, only longer, tied into a ponytail that hugged the left side of the neck.

At the bottom of the picture were three letters: ADA.

"Who is that?"

"Oh!" Gina said, startled. She looked at me, then at the mug on her desk. She took a sip. "Thank you, Cog."

"Think nothing of it."

I was pleased that we had returned to standard behavior.

I waited a moment, and when Gina did not answer my question, I again asked whose face was on the computer screen.

Gina wiped the fluid from her face.

"That's ADA," she said. "Your sister."

She pronounced it "Ayda."

I blinked, processing.

"That's how I think of you two. Brother and sister. Because I designed and built you both."

I continued to blink.

Gina's eyes continued to hydrate. She sniffed.

"Where is ADA now?" I asked.

Gina clicked her mouse, and the face disappeared. Her screen went into sleep mode. "I lost her."

I reasoned out ways ADA might have become lost if she was like me.

"I'm not going to lose you," Gina said, wiping her sleeve across her nose.

✳ ✳ ✳

The uniMIND cafeteria is a large, sunny place with light beaming down from the glass ceiling. Outside, white clouds tower like mountains against a blue sky. I feel like I want to climb them. But between me and the clouds there is glass and impossibility.

Nathan hands me an orange tray, and we go down a long counter of bins containing sausage and ham and bacon and waffles and pancakes. There are piles of bagels with tubs of butter and jam and cream cheese (which is a kind of cheese I encountered at Giganto Super Food Mart).

Nathan selects an orange and a banana and some smoked salmon with no bagel and two slices of bread that look like they have pieces of wood in them. "High fiber, low fat, and good protein, that's what I'm made of." He pats his flat stomach. "But you go ahead and pile on anything you want. You've had a few hectic days, and I bet you need to fuel up."

"At home my first biofuel of the day is most commonly cereal. Although sometimes Gina makes bacon and eggs."

"This is your home, Cog. And bacon and eggs sound good to me."

He leads me to a line where bacon and eggs are distributed and asks me how I like my eggs cooked. Cooking is when biofuels are combined, often with the addition of heat. Gina has used many different cooking methods to prepare eggs.

"I like my eggs cooked by Gina," I say.

The constant smile on Nathan's mouth falters. "Let's do scrambled," he says to the man behind the counter.

Moments later we join other uniMIND workers at a table. Nathan says hello to them and they say hello to Nathan, and then Nathan says, "This is Cog. He just arrived a few days ago, and he's going to be staying with us now."

The other workers seem friendly when they greet me. I try to seem friendly when I greet them back. They speak of things I do not know about: budgets and schedules and spreadsheets and inventories. But all the time they are watching me eat. They remind me of the way Gina observes me when I perform new tasks, such as assembling a jigsaw puzzle or figuring out how a yo-yo works. They are paying such close attention to me that I think they're trying to hear my jaw hinges whirr.

"So, Cog," says Nathan. "What can you tell us about the X-module?"

I review my memory and find that I know nothing about anything called an X-module.

He squints at me. "You must be able to tell us *something*."

I find it confusing that he wants me to give him information that I don't have, but I do my best. "Platypuses lay their eggs in watery—"

"What do platypuses have to do with the X-module?" he interrupts.

Gina never interrupts during learning sessions. I transfer a forkful of eggs into my mouth.

Nathan taps something on his tablet.

"Maybe Gina called it something else," says another uniMIND worker. She wears little round glasses that magnify her eyes.

Nathan rubs the bridge of his nose. I have learned that he does this when he is processing. "Cog, what did Gina tell you about your programming?"

This is a question I am able to answer, and I am pleased.

"She told me that I am programmed for cognitive development, and to learn by consuming information with my sensors, which are similar to human eyes, noses, ears, tongues, and skin. I am capable of learning through reading, through smelling, through hearing, through tasting—"

"This is going to take a long time," says the woman with the magnified eyes.

"—I also learn by taking risks and engaging in bad experiences. In addition, I have, at last count, seventy-three bugs. I will list them for you. One: I swallow gum. Two: I sometimes consume biofuel too quickly, which results in gas bubbles within my biofuel container. Three: I release my biofuel gas in loud eruptions that are considered non-standard. Four—"

"I think we're going to have to try another method," the woman says to Nathan.

Nathan nods and types something on his tablet. He and the woman and the other uniMIND workers engage in conversation. I continue to list my bugs, but they are not listening.

I wonder what the X-module is.

Nathan brings me to a laboratory that smells of machine oil and burning wires. Three uniMIND workers are there, drinking coffee from paper cups. One of them leans in a relaxed fashion on a hockey stick. In the center of the room stands a ladder, about my height.

"Hi, Nathan," says one of the workers, a man in a blue short-sleeved shirt tucked into tan pants. So many uniMIND employees dress this way that I am starting to have trouble telling them apart. "We were just about to run Proto through some obedience tests. Would you and Cog like to stay and watch?"

Nathan hasn't introduced me to these workers, but they know who I am. Probably everyone at uniMIND knows who I am.

"That's exactly why we're here," Nathan says. He takes my hand and leads me to the side of the room.

A worker snaps open a black plastic suitcase. Nestled inside is an object about the size of the Chihuahua from the day of rain and boogers. It is a box of metal and plastic, with exposed servos and circuit boards and bundled wires in all the colors of the rainbow.

The worker lifts the object from the case and sets it on the ground.

"Proto. Stand."

A blinking green light flashes on the front of the object, and a moment later, white-and-gray rods folded at its side extend. It stands on them like legs. Its feet are black disks like miniature shopping cart wheels, though hopefully not as buggy.

It makes a noise.

Rarf!

"This is Proto," Nathan says. "Short for 'prototype.' Do you know what a—"

I have learned to interrupt.

"A prototype is an original, or first model of something from which other forms are copied or developed."

Nathan's smile returns. "Very good, Cog."

The man with the hockey stick walks around Proto. He gently taps each of Proto's feet with the end of his stick. Then he straightens, and in a clear voice says, "Proto, climb the ladder."

Proto's green light flashes. He goes *"Rarf!"* With a whir of moving parts, he walks to the foot of the ladder. I hear hissing air.

"Proto likes to sniff before tackling a problem," Nathan says. "His nose works like yours, but while you have about six million scent receptors, Proto has three hundred million."

The hissing stops, and Proto uses his four legs to climb the rungs up the ladder. He sits on the little platform at the top, his green light blinking.

The man strikes Proto with the hockey stick. *Thwack.* Proto clatters to the ground.

"Proto, climb the ladder," he commands again.

Proto's light blinks. Again, he climbs the ladder to the top rung and sits there. Again the man strikes him with the stick and knocks Proto to the ground.

"What is the purpose of this experiment?" I ask.

"Proto, climb the ladder."

Proto climbs.

The man strikes Proto. *Thwack*. Proto falls.

"Proto is shaped like a dog, and you are shaped like a boy," Nathan says. "But underneath your syntha-derm skin, you and Proto look much alike. Isn't that interesting?"

"Yes, it is interesting. But it is not the answer to my question." Perhaps he didn't hear me over the sound of Proto hitting the ground, so I ask it again. "What is the purpose of this experiment?"

"They're testing his balance and mobility. But mostly they're testing his ability to complete tasks while faced with distractions."

I do not know what to think about Proto's balance and mobility, but as he once again reaches the top of the ladder, I conclude that he is very capable of performing despite distractions.

"How many times must Proto be struck before you have learned enough?" I ask this question not of Nathan, but of the man with the hockey stick.

He checks a piece of paper on a clipboard. "We're scheduled for seventeen more applications of stimulus."

"Does 'application of stimulus' mean hitting?"

"In this case, yes," Nathan says. "Don't worry, it doesn't hurt him."

Proto continues to climb. *Thwack.* And Proto continues to fall.

After a while, my sensors start to malfunction. My vision gets strangely sharp. I can see the tiniest of scratches in the surface of Proto's casing. With every blow of the hockey stick, there are more cracks, like fine splinters. And the noise of the impacts is too loud. Pain sensors in my head flash, as if I'm the one being hit. The feelings grow bigger, sharper. It is like being overwhelmed by cheese.

Thwack.

Thwack.

Thwack.

I am cheesing.

Thwack.

It feels like my skull is cracking.

Thwack.

And something comes out of my head. It is like light,

only I cannot see it. Nathan and the man with the hockey stick and the other workers in the room don't behave as though anything unusual is happening. Perhaps they don't see it either.

Thwack.

"Proto, climb the ladder," says the man with the hockey stick.

No.

Proto. Stop.

Stop climbing.

I do not say these words out loud. I say them only in my cheesing, cracking head.

Sprawled on the floor, Proto rights himself. He whirrs over to the ladder and puts his two front feet on the first rung. His green light blinks, and he raises a leg to continue climbing. But then he pauses. He lowers his front feet to the floor.

The pressure in my head fades.

"Proto, climb the ladder," the man with the stick says again.

Proto sits there, his rear antennae sagging.

The man frowns. He puts down his stick and comes over to examine Proto. "He seems to be functioning."

"Then why won't he run the program?" asks one of the other uniMIND workers.

Everyone looks at Proto.

Everyone but Nathan.

Nathan is looking at me.

"Cog, did you do that? Did you cause Proto to disobey his command?"

I blink, processing.

"I don't know," I say. Which is the truth.

Nathan's smile is tiny as he taps things into his notepad.

"And that, Cog, is why we need to learn about the X-module."

CHAPTER 6

I DO NOT SLEEP, but I do dream.

When I dream, it is a little like cheesing.

Here are some things I have dreamed about:

Giant Chihuahuas with truck tires instead of legs.

A world where houses and lawns and pavements are made of pizza.

Platypuses that are like mammals except they lay eggs, which is actually how platypuses really work so this dream is both realistic and strange.

Tonight, I dream of the face I saw on Gina's screen when I brought her cocoa. The face belonging to the one that Gina lost. My sister. And I say to her, "Wake up. Wake up, ADA. Wake up and run."

❁ ❁ ❁

Trashbot comes to my room to ask if I have any waste to dispose of. He always comes in the morning and again late at night before I go to bed. I do not have waste now. I almost never do. His head sags and he turns to depart and almost bumps into Nathan. Nathan tosses a coffee cup in Trashbot's waste bin. "Good morning, Cog. We've got a big day planned, so let's get moving." He seldom says anything to Trashbot.

He takes me to a lab I have not been to before. The sign on the door says "Artificial Intelligence Neuroscience Laboratory." Sharp-looking tools glint on a steel cart.

Nathan motions toward a padded chair. "Please have a seat, Cog."

It's a struggle to climb into the chair, but it's comfortable once I'm settled in. The back is high and angled, and there's enough room for me to stretch my legs.

A big screen mounted to the wall displays a diagram of a head with labeled wires and screws. It is not just any head. It is my head.

"What will I be learning today?" Despite my unease about missing Gina and witnessing Proto being struck by a hockey stick and being asked about the X-module without being told what the X-module is, I remain eager to fulfill my purpose.

A technician begins flipping up my fingernails and attaching cables.

"Today you're taking it easy," Nathan says. "Just leave the learning to us."

Technicians move around me, checking connections, doing things on computers, looking into my eyes without really looking at me.

"Is learning taking place now?" I ask.

"Don't worry, Cog," Nathan says again. "Just take it easy."

"What does it mean to take it easy?"

"It means . . . Don't do anything. Just lie there and relax."

"I am lying here. I am not doing anything. Is learning taking place?"

"We're ready," says one of the technicians. "Arrest his motor functions."

I try to turn my head to see Nathan, who has stepped out of my view, but I can't. I cannot turn my head. I cannot move my head at all. Nor my hands. Nor my arms or legs.

I try again to ask what is being learned, but I cannot move my jaw or lips.

I cannot move. I cannot speak.

"Elevated circulation pump rate," says one of the technicians.

Nathan bends over me, his face filling my vision.

"Hey, buddy, relax. This won't hurt." That is what he said when they were beating Proto with a hockey stick. He smiles down at me. "We're just going to remove your brain."

"Once your brain is out, we'll plug it into the computer and run some simulations to see how you learn under conditions of accelerated experience."

"What does that mean?" I would say if I were capable of speaking. I would also tell him that my circulation pump is beating so quickly it feels as though it might burst out of my chest.

Nathan looks at me. Not like the other technicians are looking at me, through readouts on their computers, or just seeing little bits of me one system at a time. Nathan looks like he's trying to see *me*.

"I'm sure you've got some questions. Accelerated experience means that instead of experiencing the world like you do now, in real time, from moment to moment, you'll experience hundreds of hours in seconds. Remember when you went grocery shopping?"

Nathan must have read about that in Gina's files.

"It'll be like that, but many, many times over. This way, you'll gain experience a lot faster. You'll learn a lot faster. That'll be awesome, right?"

I don't know quite what to think.

It will be good to learn faster. To learn more. To more efficiently fulfill my purpose.

But I want to experience and learn with my brain still inside my body. I want to choose where my brain resides.

"Okay, I'm ready," says a technician. "Hand me the drill, please."

Why do they need a drill? Does this have something to do with finding the X-module? If the module, whatever it is, is located inside my brain, then it makes sense to look inside the physical structure of my cognitive processor to find it.

I wonder why Nathan is not mentioning the X-module.

I think what he is doing is a form of lying.

Lying is saying something that is not true, but it is also *not* saying something that *is* true.

I wish Nathan were not lying to me.

I wish I were not here now.

I wish I were at home with Gina.

I wish I had never run into the street to save the Chihuahua.

Nathan steps away again, outside my view. All I can see is the ceiling. It is white. The lights are bright.

"Uh-oh, there's a problem," says a technician.

"What problem?" That's Nathan's voice.

"The UM-2112's malfunctioning. Give me a second. . . . Yeah. This unit's busted."

"Don't we have another drill?" Nathan asks.

"We lent it to Automotive Robotics. I can go see if they still need it."

"That's going to put us off our schedule," another technician says. "And I can't work late today. My kids have soccer practice."

There is a lot of sighing and muttering as they discuss what to do with me. None of them sound happy.

In the end, they decide to postpone removing my brain until tomorrow. By then they'll either have fixed their drill or gotten the spare drill back from the Automotive Robotics lab. They won't have to rush things. They'll have enough time to do everything they want to do to me.

My circulation pump is still beating fast.

"Sorry, Cog," Nathan says to me as they return my speech and ability to move. He begins to unplug the cables from the data ports in my fingers. He smiles. "We'll have our act together tomorrow, I promise."

The technicians are now talking about other things. Other projects. What they're going to have for lunch. Their kids and soccer. They don't seem to remember I'm here until Nathan tells me to get up.

"I do not wish to have my brain removed," I say as Nathan walks me back to my room.

"Cog, I told you it won't hurt. And it'll only be out for a little while."

"I understand. I do not wish to have my brain removed."

Nathan's smile is tight.

"Look, you just get some rest and take it easy."

"I do not wish to rest. I do not wish to take it easy. I do

not wish to have my brain removed."

He starts to tell me again how painless it will be.

"Nathan, if I told you I was going to remove your brain with a drill, and that it would only be outside of your skull for a short time, and that it would be painless, would you want me to do it?"

"That's an entirely different thing, Cog."

We reach my room. Nathan opens the door for me.

"How is it different?"

"In more ways than I can count. Get in."

I step inside and he closes the door. The lock buzzes and hums.

I try the knob. It doesn't move.

I am locked inside.

I have been hit by a truck and separated from Gina and I have lost my home and been strapped to a chair without the ability to speak or move. Of all those things, being locked in my room is not the worst.

But it is enough to push me into formulating a plan.

I am going to leave uniMIND.

In order to do that, I will require an accomplice.

An accomplice is someone who helps you perform a task that is against the rules.

I have already decided who my accomplice will be.

Together, we will exercise poor judgment and have bad experiences and learn things.

My accomplice is very lucky, I feel.

CHAPTER 7

WHEN TRASHBOT COMES TO MY room late at night to ask his usual question, I give him something other than my usual answer.

"Yes, I do have waste to dispose of."

Trashbot's faceplate lights up green. He rolls back a few inches and then forward. He raises his arms and clenches his graspers. I think he's excited.

"Please direct me to your waste," he says.

"It's not here. It is elsewhere in the complex."

I am not saying anything that is untrue, but I am leaving out things that *are* true. I am lying. I find it surprisingly easy to do this. I wonder if my ability to lie is part of the X-module.

"Trashbot, do you have access to all parts of campus? And can you select routes that avoid encounters with uni-MIND employees?"

His face blinks green. I take it as a yes.

"Then lead me to the laboratory where Proto is stored."

He rolls down the corridor, and before I close the door behind me, I take a last glance into my room. I see the books Gina gave me, sitting in straight, organized rows. I see my posters of spacecraft and dinosaurs on the walls and my models hanging from the ceiling with fishing line. I see my stars.

These were my things when I lived with Gina. But somehow, once transported to this room at uniMIND, they stopped being my things. They are like me. I was myself with Gina. Here, I am property.

I close the door and resolve to never come back.

The route to Proto takes us into janitorial supply rooms, toilet stalls, the cafeteria kitchen, and a room with a Ping-Pong table. The building is quiet at night, fortunately, and by pausing before turning corners and crouching behind water fountains and diving behind potted plants, I manage to avoid being spotted by uniMIND workers. Trashbot doesn't have to bother with that. People are used to seeing him all over campus.

"Where is the waste you wish to dispose of?" Trashbot asks when we arrive at Proto's lab.

The ladder is still in the middle of the floor. The hockey stick the uniMIND worker used to hit Proto leans against Proto's case.

"You can have the stick," I tell Trashbot.

Trashbot races over and picks up the stick with his graspers. There's a violent grinding noise as he feeds it into his waste bin. A wisp of wood dust twirls in the air before Trashbot vacuums it up.

Nobody will ever hit Proto with that particular hockey stick again.

Meanwhile, I snap open the case and lift Proto out of it. I find the "On" switch under his belly. Proto's lights flash green. He stretches his legs and wags his antennae.

"Proto, I am escaping uniMIND. Would you like to come with me?"

"*Rarf,*" Proto responds.

"Good. Trashbot, there's more waste to dispose of in the Automotive Robotics Laboratory."

Trashbot flashes green and leads the way.

✳ ✳ ✳

The Automotive Robotics Laboratory is a dim under-ground parking garage. Bare cement walls echo every sound we make, from the rumble and whir of Trashbot's treads to the squeaks of my sneakers.

A variety of vehicles fills the space. I think most of them are tanks. There is also something that looks like a cross between a bicycle and a helicopter studded with carrot-sized missiles. In the shadows looms a giant spider with a seat on top, and parked next to it is a single wheel with what appear to be steak knives poking out of it.

I spot the vehicle that most closely resembles the van Gina drove. It's a car painted in a kind of black that does not reflect light. Its windows are darkened, and it is low to the ground with big chunky tires, and it really doesn't resemble Gina's van much at all. But at least there are no steak knives.

"This way, Proto."

I creep between other vehicles to the black car. Creep-ing seems like a good idea because I do not wish to attract the attention of anyone who might interfere with my attempt to escape.

But a noise attracts *my* attention: footsteps clicking hard on the concrete floor.

I crouch low, hiding behind the bumper of a truck that

looks like scissors with wheels. Trashbot cannot crouch, and Proto does not need to, but they are both capable of making noise, and if they do, our presence will be detected. I will end up back in a chair with my skull drilled open.

The footsteps tap ever closer. A flashlight beam crawls along the wall behind us.

It lands on Trashbot's faceplate.

In the side mirror of the truck, I spot the reflection of a worker in a dark blue uniform with the uniMIND logo stitched on her jacket. A security guard. Is Trashbot allowed in the Automotive Robotics Laboratory alone?

"Do you have any waste you wish to dispose of?" Trashbot's voice thunders in the dark space.

"Nope," says the guard. "I ate a burrito a while ago. That's the good thing about burritos. Nothing to throw away. You don't need a fork and knife or anything. Not even a plate. The tortilla *is* the plate. Isn't that brilliant?"

What did she do with the wrapper? Perhaps she ate it.

Trashbot apparently has no opinions regarding the brilliance of burritos. The security guard sighs. Her footsteps recede into the distance, and then there is silence.

Burritos *are* somewhat brilliant, I think.

And, in his own way, perhaps Trashbot is brilliant, too.

Were it not for him I would still be locked in my room.

"Trashbot," I whisper, "would you like to join Proto and me for bad experiences? There will likely be much waste along the way."

Trashbot says nothing, but when I move to the car I have selected for our escape, he trundles along behind me.

"UNAUTHORIZED PRESENCE," blares a voice.

My circulation pump thumps so hard it feels like it's lodged in my throat. I touch both my chest and my throat to confirm that all my body parts are where they're supposed to be.

A robot rolls out between two of the parked vehicles. It is configured much like Trashbot, only its faceplate is red like a stop light and it does not have a waste bin in the middle and instead of two arms it has six arms and instead of graspers it has sharp pokey things on the ends of its appendages. It is also twice as tall as Trashbot. It towers over us, loud and buzzy.

"UNAUTHORIZED PRESENCE. PREPARE TO BE RESTRAINED."

"Do you have any waste to dispose of?" says Trashbot.

"I do not think it has any waste, Trashbot."

Trashbot's head dips. "I was promised waste."

The robot raises its arms. Blue lightning sizzles around its grabbers, and with a clanking sound, it rolls toward us on its tank treads.

"PREPARE TO BE RESTRAINED. DAMAGE MAY OCCUR."

The robot is between us and the car. I do not wish to be restrained and I do not want to be damaged, but if I have learned one thing since I arrived at uniMIND, it's that nobody cares what I want.

I do a word problem.

Can a biomaton in the form of a ninety-pound boy and a prototype dog and a janitorial robot overpower an armed security robot?

The answer is obviously no.

But there is one thing I did not count on.

The security robot's head comes off in a dazzling shower of sparks. With creaking and groaning metal, it teeters forward, rocking a little bit before tipping over and slamming on the concrete floor. It lies there, severed wires spitting electric blue.

In its place stands a girl, still holding the security robot's head. She is a little taller than me, a little heavier than me, skin a little lighter than mine. I recognize her blunt nose and square chin and brown eyes. I have seen her face before, on Gina's computer screen, when I brought Gina hot cocoa and Gina's eyes were well lubricated.

"ADA," I say. "You are my sister."

She blinks at me.

"I am escaping, ADA. Are you escaping as well?"

"I suppose."

"I am Cog."

"Okay," she says.

And then we are just standing here, blinking at each other. ADA still has a robot head in her hands.

The robot head makes a little noise out of its voice box.

It sounds like "Uuuuuuugh."

"Hey!" the security guard screams, running back over. "You kids . . . robots . . . whatever. Hold it right there!"

"I am planning to make my escape by means of this car," I inform ADA. "Would you like to join me?"

"Why not take one of armored assault vehicles studded with missiles?"

"Don't you feel that will attract attention outside the uniMIND campus?"

"I am unconcerned about attracting attention," ADA says.

The guard is almost upon us now and is speaking into a walkie-talkie. She is saying things like "out of her cage" and "wrecked a security bot" and "the boy's out too."

"I think the car would be a better choice," I tell ADA.

"I will go along with your choice. But if you are wrong, there will be . . . consequences."

We pile into the car, me in the driver's seat with Proto in my lap, ADA beside me, and Trashbot in the back seat.

"Do you know how to drive?" ADA asks.

"I have seen it done before."

"Does that mean yes or no?"

"Yes, it means either yes or no."

ADA blinks at me.

I press the big round green button on the dashboard, hoping it will start the engine.

"Programming is thirty percent complete," says a voice. "Do you wish to operate me before full programming?"

"Yes," I say.

"Do you accept full liability for any damage caused by operating me before full programming is complete?"

I remember Gina talking about liability one time when she was on the phone to the insurance company after I started a kitchen fire by trying to dry my clothes in the oven. "Liability" means that everything is your fault.

The security guard is pulling my door handle and banging on the window, demanding that we get out of the vehicle.

"I accept liability," I say.

"State destination," says the car.

"Take us to the highway, please. Maximum speed."

Maximum speed turns out to be very fast.

With a screech of tires on concrete, the car backs out of the parking space. The security guards jumps away, barely avoiding impact, and in an instant we are thundering down the floor of the garage. Directly toward a metal gate blocking the exit.

"Barrier detected," the car says.

"Drive through it," ADA commands.

"Do you wish to accept full liability for any damage incurred by a collision?"

I look behind us. The security guard is running to catch up, still screaming into her walkie-talkie.

"Yes, Cog will accept liability," ADA tells the car.

And so, with the roar of a very powerful engine, the car accelerates toward the metal barrier.

I don't think ADA cares what "liability" means.

CHAPTER 8

LATER, AFTER THE CAR HAS crashed through the
security barrier, sped down the roads of the uniMIND
campus, and swerved and bounced and zigzagged to the
highway, we assess our damage.

The pain sensors in my back and neck are in the yellow
from being thrown around the car.

Proto has a small dent in his head from when the car
went up a curb and Proto flew into the dashboard.

ADA is undamaged.

Trashbot is undamaged.

The car is undamaged.

"Please state your destination," the car says.

"Wait," ADA says. She gets down on the passenger seat

floorboard and probes under the dashboard. There is an alarming, plasticky cracking sound, and she comes up with a little silver box trailing severed wires.

"This is a tracking device," she says. "I have damaged it so that we will not be tracked."

"You will have to accept liability for that damage," the car says.

ADA yanks the wires out and tosses them in the back seat. Trashbot eats them.

"Car . . . I do not know what to call you. I am Cog."

"I am Car. Please state your destination."

Nathan told me Gina was transferred to a different uni-MIND facility, one far from me, but I know she would not stay there. She would go home. She would repair her broken heart and wait for me to return.

I give Car the address of the house where I lived with Gina.

"Please obey all traffic laws. You are currently travel-ing forty miles per hour over the speed limit."

Car does not slow down. Fortunately, at 12:43 a.m., traffic is light, and so we have not yet experienced a fiery collision.

"Car . . . ?"

"I am considering your request."

ADA leans back in her seat and begins to explore the pop-out cup holders. "I am comfortable traveling at this speed."

Proto curls up in my lap and enters sleep mode.

"Do you have any waste you wish to dispose of?" says Trashbot from the back seat.

Clearly, I am the only one here who has ever been seriously damaged in a high-speed impact.

"Traveling more slowly will increase the likelihood of successfully reaching our destination," I say.

Car continues speeding along for another quarter mile, but then slows to the speed limit, and so we are not crushed or mangled or incinerated when Car pulls off the highway and navigates the curving, tree-lined streets.

Gina's house is dark when we roll up the driveway. Even the porch light is inactivated.

I tell Proto and ADA and Trashbot to remain in Car while I go to the door. They refuse my request and accompany me up the porch.

"What is this place?" asks ADA.

I turn to her, confused.

"Did you never live here with Gina?"

"All my time with Gina was at uniMIND headquarters. I have spent my whole life there. This is my first time outside."

She looks at the sky glittering with stars. Her nostrils flare, and I wonder if she is taking in the scent of the eucalyptus trees in the neighbor's backyard. I wonder what is going on in her brain right now. I wonder if she is cheesing.

I try to turn the doorknob.

"It is locked."

"Stand back," ADA instructs. Before I can ask her why, she raises her foot and drives it into the door. Metal cracks and wood splinters, and the door hangs on one broken hinge.

"The door is no longer locked," ADA says.

I am built for cognitive development. I am not certain what ADA is built for. Later, I will ask her, but now I am anxious to see Gina, so I step inside.

There is no puffy sofa in the living room where Gina and I would watch comedies and she would try to explain to me why they were funny.

No TV mounted on the wall. No table where we used to put our big box of pizza or bowls of buttered popcorn. In the kitchen, the plates and bowls and mixer and toaster are gone. There is no biofuel in the refrigerator. There is no toilet paper in the bathroom. No soap. No scented candles. In my bedroom there is only bare carpet

The house is empty.

It is all empty.

And Gina is nowhere to be found. It's as if she never lived here. As if she's been deleted.

"Is this not what you expected?" ADA asks me, peering inside the closet that used to contain raincoats and umbrellas but now contains only a single dust bunny and an extension cord connected to nothing.

Trashbot vacuums up the dust bunny and draws the extension cord into his bin like a spaghetti noodle.

"I thought Gina would still be here. I thought I could tell her what happened to me at uniMIND. I thought I could tell her what I have learned since getting hit by the truck." I look at the blank, white walls. "I thought I could come home."

I exit the house, go down the porch, cross the front yard, get back into Car. None of these moves feel like deliberate decisions. I'm just walking. I'm just moving.

CHAPTER 9

CAR CHOOSES HER OWN DIRECTION. She takes us east, away from everything I have known and toward experiences I can't predict. My mind occupies a place between.

I need a library.

A library is a place where information can be found, and finding information is a way to increase cognitive development. The specific information I require is Gina's current location. So I must learn where other uniMIND facilities are located.

It's almost noon when Car finally comes to a stop. The library is a one-story building of red brick in a town with a lot of lawns and parks. I ask Proto and Trashbot and

ADA to stay in Car while I go learn, but ADA exits the vehicle and strides toward the entrance.

"Will there be any waste to dispose of?" Trashbot asks.

"I don't think so."

Trashbot's faceplate dims, and he remains in the back seat.

Proto *rarfs* and curls up into a ball beside him.

Inside, floor-to-ceiling windows let in light. ADA stands in the middle of the floor, eyes narrowed, and turns around in a slow circle. "Threat assessment is low," she says. "But I suppose we should try not to attract notice."

"That may be difficult. We are the physical size and appearance of children, and there are times when it is non-standard for children to be without adult supervision. It is now noon, a time when most children are at school."

ADA blinks for a moment. "There are many books here. Books are flammable. If we are challenged I can pull off one of my fingers to expose raw wires and generate a spark, which, combined with a book, will start a fire. The fire will serve as a diversion should we need to make an escape."

"Good," I tell ADA, though I hope we will not have to

burn the library down.

An adult enters the library with twenty children in tow. The children carry backpacks and are all dressed alike, in gray pants or skirts and blue shirts, some with blue sweaters as well. They talk and laugh until the adult says, "Library rules," and soon the children are quiet and whispering.

ADA tenses. "Is this some kind of military unit?"

"I don't think so."

"But they are wearing uniforms."

"I believe they are school uniforms. See, the ones with sweaters have patches that say 'Grassville Elementary School.' This is a school class, and they have come to the library to do . . . school things."

"School things?"

"Yes. School is one way in which humans increase their cognitive development."

The teacher gives them instructions. They are to find books on topics related to the way mountains and canyons are formed. The children—students—begin to wander among the shelves. I have a very strong desire to join them and learn about mountain and canyon formation. I want to do school things.

"We are not dressed like them," ADA says, "but perhaps the presence of other children will make us less noticeable."

A sweater-wearing girl stares at us while she pulls a book off a shelf.

"Maybe," I say.

At the computer station I begin my search by typing "uniMIND facilities."

"That says 7,852,000 results," ADA says.

I blink at ADA. "I did not know you have learned how to read."

"I didn't learn. I was programmed with reading ability."

"Oh. I had to learn."

"That's because you're built for learning. I am built to be offensive. How are you going to find the information you seek out of so many search results?"

The answer seems obvious to me, but perhaps ADA does not think the same way I do. "I'm going to read them."

"All of them?"

"If necessary."

"We will be here for years."

"I read quickly."

"You can't read that quickly."

I turn to the screen. "Witness me."

I only need to read the first result to find out what I'm looking for. It is uniMIND's main website, and it lists all the locations where they have facilities. There is the campus we came from in California. The next closest is in Germany, which is across an entire continent and an entire ocean. After the German location, the next closest is in China, which is even farther. They are both many thousands of miles away.

"ADA, do you think Car can fly?"

"No, I do not."

"What about travel over water?"

"I would not trust Car to drive through a deep puddle."

My biofuel container goes cold and heavy. My hopes of finding Gina shrink.

I do not know what to do. So, I rely on my purpose. I learn.

Scrolling through several pages of results, my eyes land on one that is different. It is a newspaper article titled "Does uniMIND Have a Secret Facility?"

I click the link and find myself staring at a photograph of a bald man with a red face smiling so broadly all his teeth are showing. The text beneath the picture says "Hank Guff, Former uniMIND Employee."

The first line of the article is a quote from Hank Guff: "It all started with the pigs."

Reading on, I learn things.

I learn that Hank Guff was something called a "form processor" at uniMIND, and that he really loves pigs. He decorated his entire workspace with pigs. Pig calendars. Pig coffee mugs. Pig figurines. Pig stickers. Many, many pigs, on every surface available to him.

One day, his uniMIND supervisor told him he had to get rid of his pigs.

"It made no sense," Guff says in the article. "The pigs weren't hurting anyone. They weren't preventing me from doing my job. I was still processing my 1080 TPBs on time, and my RUXP-R1ENSTs were cleaner than anyone in the whole department. What's my pigs got to do with any-thing?"

The article says Guff's supervisor claimed his pigs vio-lated corporate culture.

"Corporate culture?" Hank says. "What's that? I mean, I know what culture is. It's the food that comes from the country where you or your ancestors immigrated from. Or it's music and art, like, paintings and stuff. But if uni-MIND's culture forbids harmless little pig toys, then I don't want no part of it. Everybody thinks uniMIND is this perfect place to work. Everyone's friendly there, as long as you look the way they want you to look and act the way they want you to act. Just obey, and you'll be fine. But step out of line—like, for instance, with a pig-a-day calendar—and all of a sudden they're roasting you on the spit. And that's just the California campus. I hear there's worse. They got a secret place on Hogan's Island. It's private property and you can't even land on the shore without uniMIND's say-so. They call it the Tower. Nobody even knows what they do out there. But I bet it's spooky. I bet they got a lot of corporate culture, and no pigs allowed."

"Cog, that human girl has been watching us since we sat down," ADA says. "I assess her as a threat."

I look up. The girl who was staring at us before is still staring at us. She is still removing the same book from the shelf she was removing before, as if frozen.

"She is probably just curious. I sometimes stare at people when I am curious, even though Gina instructed me that staring is a form of nonstandard behavior called rudeness."

"I am going to eliminate her," ADA says, taking a step.

"ADA, that will attract attention."

"In that case I will execute my plan of pulling off my finger and burning down the library."

"It seems like you just want to destroy the library."

"Don't you?"

I blink at her.

"I was built for violence. ADA stands for Advanced Destructive Apparatus. Or Assault Deployment Array. Actually, I'm not sure what ADA stands for. But it's probably something like that. I am a weapon."

"I believe we should take a different course of action."

ADA pauses, gripping her index finger with the opposite hand. "Yes?"

"I want to find the secret tower."

CHAPTER 10

HOGAN'S ISLAND IS IN OHIO, halfway across the country, in the middle of Lake Erie. If we don't stop for fuel, food, sleep, or restroom breaks, it will take us thirty-eight hours to get to the Tower.

ADA has spent the first six hours of our journey complaining that she is hungry: "I used energy during our escape, and I have not consumed biofuel since I was last put into sleep mode."

Proto *rarf*s, and a sound comes from deep inside Trashbot that's similar to the rumble my biofuel container makes when it is empty. Which it is now.

I try to stay encouraging. "We're almost there. Just hold on for another 2,155 miles."

The streets and neighborhoods on Car's dashboard map display look like the little curls of a human brain. Ahead of us is a vast expanse of green. There are very few dots to indicate habitations. We've been going uphill for a while, and the rising sun casts rays between tree trunks wide enough for Car to drive through. I think of the elevator shaft tree at uniMIND headquarters and wonder if there are people inside the trees.

"I'm hungry," ADA says.

She says it another fifteen times before we come upon a town named Pine Grove Meadow Falls. According to the sign on the edge of town, Pine Grove Meadow Falls sits at an elevation of 5,420 feet above sea level. The population of Pine Grove Meadow Falls is 456 people. The motto of Pine Grove Meadow Falls is "Welcome to Pine Grove Meadow Falls."

We almost drive through Pine Grove Meadow Falls because Car does not slow down from highway speed until ADA threatens to rip her engine out.

Car slows down.

"Where is the biofuel in this place stored?" ADA's voice is very loud. Perhaps being hungry has put her into what Gina would call a "foul mood."

"Biofuel can be purchased at markets and restaurants."

"Locate one of these . . . markets and restaurants," she says.

I remember that she has spent her entire life at uni-MIND headquarters. She has never been to Giganto Super Food Mart. Or the Beef Hut drive-through. Or Pancake Palace. Or Wild Waffles. She has never been anywhere.

I spot a restaurant with a sign shaped like a large hot dog. Artificial trees rise from it with artificial snow dusting the boughs. Letters spell out "Wiener Mountain, Home of the Wiener Mountain."

I tell Car to park.

"This is a source of biofuel?" ADA asks.

"Yes. It is a form of biofuel called hot dogs. It is very good biofuel. We just need money to pay for it. It is standard." I search Car and find some money in a tray underneath the radio. "This is money," I explain to ADA, showing her several small, metal disks in my hand. "Money can be exchanged for things. Biofuel is among the things money can be exchanged for."

"How much money is that?"

I count the coins. "Six thousand and three dollars."

ADA blinks. "Is that a lot?"

"Stand by. I have made an error. I am recounting. Stand by. Correction: This is sixty-three cents."

ADA blinks. "Is that a lot?"

Inside, a man wearing a T-shirt and white apron chews a toothpick behind the counter. He has more hair on his forearms than ADA and I have on our heads combined. He doesn't say anything for a minute.

He takes the toothpick out of his mouth and sets it down on the counter. "That one of those vacuum cleaners?"

I don't know which one of us he thinks is a vacuum cleaner.

"Do you have any waste you wish to dispose of?" asks Trashbot.

"Trashbot is not a vacuum cleaner," I inform the man.

"What about that one?" He points to Proto.

"Proto is a dog," I tell him.

"*Rarf,*" Proto says.

"Huh, cute," the man says. "Kinda." He returns the toothpick to his mouth. "What can I get you?"

"What is the most amount of food we can have for the least amount of money?"

"Well, now," he says. "You can get a Mini Mountain for a buck."

I know from having learned many things about animals that a buck is a male deer. Deer are cloven-hoofed ungulates with good nighttime vision. All male deer grow antlers, except for Chinese water deer. I know many other facts about deer, but it is unclear to me how we are to obtain a male deer in order to exchange it for a hot dog. Perhaps the man in the apron understands even less about money than I do.

"We had hoped to exchange money for biofuel," I explain to him with great patience.

"You talk funny," he says. "Where you from?"

"We are from California."

"That explains it."

ADA and I blink at him.

"You can get a Mini Mountain for a dollar," he says. "You know what a dollar is? A hundred cents?"

"I do know what a dollar is," I inform him. "We do not have a hundred cents."

"Heh, you kids and your toys are adorable. Tell you what. Go away." He inserts a second toothpick between his teeth and gnaws.

I turn to leave, but then I spot a sign on the wall: "CON-QUER WIENER MOUNTAIN, WIN FREE T-SHIRT, EAT FOR FREE."

"*Free* means something that doesn't require money, correct?"

"Yeah, so?"

"We wish to conquer Wiener Mountain."

Twenty minutes later, the man sets a platter bearing two hot dogs on the table with a heavy *klunk*. He winces and stretches his back.

ADA and I blink at the Wiener Mountains, processing. The wieners are the size of fire extinguishers, nestled in giant, pillowy buns. They're topped with shovelfuls of chili, gallons of liquid cheese, mounds of onions, and heaps of relish. I worry about the table's ability to support their weight.

The man produces a stopwatch from his pocket. The case is stained with spots of brown crust that I believe is chili. "Here's the deal. You have fifteen minutes to eat the mountains. No sharing. If you clean your plates, you eat free. You each get a T-shirt. You get your pictures on the Wall of Fame. That's bragging rights. Glory. Immortality.

But if you don't finish? No glory. No fame. And you pay. If you try to eat and run? Then you'll be talking to Carl."

"Who is Carl?" ADA asks.

He points to the wall on which hangs a baseball bat with a small brass plate beneath it. The plate says "Carl." The bat, like the stopwatch, has brown stains, but I do not think the stains are chili.

"I am unafraid of Carl," ADA announces.

The man just smiles. He clicks the watch. "Go."

There is a tick for every second that passes, but even after thirty ticks, I have not begun eating.

It is standard to eat hot dogs with one's hands, but the mountains are far too large to pick up. Eating with utensils, such as knife and fork, is another standard way to consume biofuel, but we have not been provided any tools.

ADA has begun eating by bending forward, smashing her face into the mountain toppings, and furiously biting. This is a nonstandard method, and I cannot see that she is making any progress, but at least she is eating.

I begin employing her nonstandard method.

For the first five minutes, my mastication plates do not contact wiener or bun. There is only chili and cheese and onions and relish. I have already had enough. My biofuel container is almost full. I cannot catch my breath. I have biofuel all over my face and in my hair and on my shirt.

ADA is doing better. Her mouth opens and shuts at a blurring speed. I wonder if her jaw is equipped with its own engine. Perhaps its own brain.

I do not know if I can go on. I certainly cannot finish my entire Wiener Mountain. But the stopwatch continues to tick away.

I glance up from a sea of chili and see the man with his arms crossed, scowling at us. He has moved closer to Carl.

Failing to finish means we have to pay.

Failing to pay means Carl.

So, I eat.

And eat.

And eat.

And I learn things.

Here are some of the things I learn:

It is possible to have too much of a good thing.

Getting what you thought you wanted can be painful. Physically painful.

I do not like chili dogs.

I do not like chili.

I do not like food.

ADA licks the last residues of mountain off her plate. She is frightening and impressive. I am neither.

Tick, tick, tick goes the stopwatch.

The watch echoes. The fluids in my head echo. ADA's voice echoes. She is threatening to do things to me if I don't conquer the mountain. They involve removal of my head and limbs and internal devices.

I eat. I eat and eat and eat. Dark shadows flicker in the corner of my vision, tunneling, closing in. I think I am dying.

The ticking finally stops.

"Aaaaand, fifteen minutes!" the man says.

We have only sixty-three cents. We cannot pay. We will have to flee with a large quantity of Wiener Mountain inside me, which is stealing.

We will have to talk to Carl.

The man strikes my back, and I brace for assault. But he is not attacking me. He is congratulating me.

"You did it! You conquered the mountain! Both of you!"

Before, he seemed hostile and dangerous. Now, he exhibits emotions I would describe as surprise and delight. He calls people from the kitchen, and he's clapping and cheering and menacing anyone in Wiener Mountain who is not joining in.

I look down at my tray. There are only the thinnest smears of food grease left.

I did it.

Through this negative experience, I have learned that I am capable of more than I thought.

I do not know if learning this lesson is worth it, because my biofuel container is filled with food and pain.

ADA drags her finger through the grease on my tray and licks it.

The man presents us with two clean, white T-shirts that say "I Conquered the Mountain at Wiener Mountain."

He shoos us off to the restrooms to change into them. It feels good to get out of my food-soggy shirt and into the T-shirt.

When ADA and I return from changing, he poses us with our defeated trays and takes our picture.

We have achieved fame, glory, and immortality.

Later, after we have left, I throw up a great deal of fame, glory, and immortality on the highway.

CHAPTER 11

WE HAVE BEEN ON THE road for fourteen hours now. The man at Wiener Mountain gave us a couple of Mini Mountains for the road, which we gladly gave to Proto, so his biofuel container is satisfied. He sticks his head out the window as Car speeds down from the mountains toward a broad, sandy plain below. The wind blasts air in his face, but he doesn't seem to mind. In fact, if his constant *rarf*ing is any indication, he likes it. The fresh air also helps with the unpleasant odors filling Car. The odors are from ADA and me, and we are producing them as a result of having quickly consumed Wiener Mountains. Our biofuel containers are holding more biofuel than they're designed to, and we are releasing waste products in gas form.

"Do you have any waste you wish to dispose of?" Trashbot says.

"I do not believe that would be a good idea right now, Trashbot."

Trashbot does not know how to respond to this, so Trashbot just makes a clacking sound, as if he is trying to chew without having anything to chew.

"Car, roll up windows," ADA says.

Car complies and the windows whir up.

"Why did you do that?" I inquire of ADA.

"Dirt particles were hitting my face."

"Thank you for answering. Car, roll windows down."

Car complies and the windows whir down.

"Why did you do that?" ADA inquires of me.

"Don't you find the smells we are producing unpleasant?"

"I do not," ADA says. "I switched off my scent detectors."

"You can turn off your sense of smell?"

She looks at me with an expression I read as surprise. "Can't you?"

"No. What else can you turn off?"

"I can turn off all my sensory detectors. Smell, sight, sound, pain . . ."

I remember lying in the road after being hit by the pickup truck, wishing I could shut my pain sensors off.

"I wonder why you were constructed with this ability and I was not."

"The purpose of pain is to tell you something is wrong. That you are damaged. But if I am damaged, pain can prevent me from continuing to fulfill my purpose. By shutting off my pain sensors, I can continue to fight."

I process this as the mountain pine trees give way to scrub.

"What is your purpose?"

"As I told you," ADA says, "I am a weapon. I am offensive."

The wind whips hair into my face, and Proto *rarfs* out the window.

"I regret that having the windows open blows dirt particles into your face."

"It is no matter," ADA says. "I have turned off the ability to feel in my face."

I pull Proto back all the way inside the car.

"Car, roll windows back up."

For some reason, I find it better to suffer the discomfort of bad smells than to make ADA prevent herself from feeling.

"ADA, you can return feeling to your face. I will leave the windows up."

After a long time during which I assume she is processing on her own, she says, "Thank you, Cog."

I continue to suffer from bad smells, but they don't bother me as much as before.

As the buildings of a distant city shimmer on the approaching horizon, an airy hiss attracts my attention. At first I think it's coming from ADA, but I do not detect the scent of biowaste. Then a rough flapping noise joins the hissing, and Car judders and bucks like the time I bathed myself in the washing machine, which is an unintelligent machine designed for washing fabrics, not robots.

"I have a flat tire," Car reports. "It is your fault."

"How far can you continue with a flat tire?" I ask.

"I'm not going any farther. I'm done." Car pulls to the side of the road, comes to a complete stop, and sits there, stubborn.

"How long will it take us to walk to Hogan's Island?" ADA wants to know.

I have no intention of walking to Hogan's Island, but I do the calculation anyway just to learn the answer. "Not counting stops for rest, biofueling, biowaste elimination, getting run over by pickup trucks due to the picking of desiccated nasal particles . . . Approximately twenty-seven days."

"Or you could just change my tire," Car suggests. "There should be a spare in my rear storage compartment."

ADA gets out and walks around to Car's rear compartment. She peers inside for a moment and says, "There is a toolbox and an empty coffee cup but no tire. The contents of your rear compartment are useless."

"Can I have the coffee cup?" Trashbot asks.

ADA feeds it to him.

If we have to walk all the way to Hogan's Island, we are sure to have bad experiences and learning opportunities. I am a little bit pleased by the prospect of learning, but I am impatient to get to the Tower in hopes of reuniting with Gina.

We have no choice. We will have to go into the city and fix Car's tire.

I learn the following things from pushing Car:

1. ADA is strong and good at pushing things.

2. I am less strong and not good at pushing things.

3. Trashbot's arms are very bad at pushing things.

4. Proto likes to chase bugs.

Road gravel crunches beneath our feet, and we say nothing until we arrive at a combination gas station, auto mechanic's garage, and convenience store. Dozens of cars are stopped here like animals gathering at a waterhole on the dry savannah. Tired-looking adults pump gas or try to herd arguing children into the convenience store.

ADA and I push Car up to the garage and go inside. Proto scampers before us, zooming between metal tool chests and cars lifted up on hoists. His foot pods splash in the inch of water covering the cement floor, and while it seems strange to me that there's so much water, this is my first time in a mechanic's shop. Perhaps this is standard. A burned and blackened rag floats by my feet. Perhaps this, too, is standard. But ADA says, "I believe a terrible battle was waged here. Though I see no bodies, many combatants must have fallen. We should be on our guard or else whatever befell the warriors will doom us."

"I'm the one who's doomed," wails a voice. A young

woman emerges from a side office, her gray coveralls soaked from the knees down. Shiny patches of oil smudge her brown cheeks. She appears to have recently had a bad experience.

"Did you exercise bad judgment?" I ask her.

"You could say that." Her voice shudders. "It all started when I flushed the toilet. Our plumbing's awful, and you never know what's going to happen, but you *have* to flush, right? Otherwise it's gross, and then you're like Floyd. He's my boss, and he's gross. Anyway, the toilet backed up and started gushing all over the place and I sort of panicked and just stared at it instead of turning the shut-off valve, and that's when the shop got flooded. Then I lit a match because watching flames sort of calms me, you know? Once the match was out I threw it in the garbage can, except the match wasn't all the way out, I guess, and there were a bunch of oily rags in the can and they ignited and all of a sudden the *whole can was on fire!* I went running for the fire extinguisher but instead ran right into the garbage can and toppled it over, and the standing water on the floor put out the fire. So I guess maybe it was good that the toilet backed up? I don't even know anymore. I just want to sit down in a dark room and light a match."

I blink for a good, long time. Then I ask, "What did you learn?"

"If I don't get this all cleaned up, I'm going to learn what it's like to lose my job."

Proto *rarfs* and goes paddling by.

"Can you repair our tire before you lose your job? We have sixty-three cents."

The mechanic laughs, but it is not a sound that expresses humor, happiness, or mirth.

"I don't think we will successfully repair or replace Car's tire here," I inform ADA.

But then Trashbot trundles up beside me. "Do you have any waste you wish to dispose of?"

The mechanic's laugh rises higher in pitch. It is a little bit like a scream. "Why, yes, I do. This whole shop is a waste. My life is a waste. Everything is waste."

Trashbot's faceplate flashes green. "Affirmative," he says. A hose spools out of a compartment on the front of his body. He submerges the end of the hose in the water and begins vibrating with a mechanical noise. The water gloops and shlorps and ripples, and when Proto begins fighting the current to keep from being drawn to the hose, I realize Trashbot is vacuuming up the water.

Proto *rarfs* as I pick him up and *rarfs* a little more angrily as I shake water off of him. Trashbot continues rolling around the garage, and gradually the water level goes down until there are only puddles here and there, and even these, Trashbot takes care of. He's only getting started.

He picks up the burned and oily rags and turns the fallen garbage can upright. Next, a panel on his back opens to reveal a fine-mesh grill. He makes a rumbling, whirring noise, and after several minutes the air smells less like burned oil and smoke.

"It will take me approximately sixteen minutes to heat-dry the area," he announces. "This will prevent the development of mold and mildew." Casting a bright orange light from his faceplate, he travels around the garage, shining his face light along the way.

I find I cannot look away from him. I am learning so much about Trashbot. For one thing, I learn that Trashbot is *really* good at his job.

Finally, Trashbot trundles back over to us. The garage is dry, clean, and smells like a fresh spring breeze. "A tidy world, brought to you by uniMIND," he says.

The mechanic is smiling and crying at the same time. I do not know what this collision of emotions means, but she wipes her hands on her pants and says, "Bring me that punctured tire. I'm gonna fix it for you. And you can keep your sixty-three cents."

The mechanic directs Trashbot to a ditch behind the garage where he can empty his internal water tank while ADA and I make for the restrooms in the convenience store. Much like Trashbot, we are full of waste, though in our case it is biowaste left over from Wiener Mountain.

I have never been inside a convenience store, so I pause to learn what it is like. Racks of food items and medications fill brightly lit aisles, very much like the Giganto Super Food Mart, only smaller and more squished together. Children gather before displays of candy bars and gum and fill paper buckets with colorful carbonated liquids.

What are their lives like? I wonder. Do they live in homes like the one I shared with Gina? Do they go to school? Have they ever had their brains removed with a drill? I decide the best way to learn is by asking them, so I take a step toward the soda fountain. ADA stops me by grabbing my arm. She has a very strong grip.

"ADA, you are interfering with my cognitive development. Let go."

ADA does not let go. She points to the cash registers. Taped to the wall is a sheet of paper, and printed on the paper in large type is the word "MISSING." Two photographs sit below the type. One of them is a photograph of ADA. Beside it is a photograph of me. Written descriptions accompany the photographs. They include height and weight and hair and eye color and clothing. At the bottom of the paper is a phone number with instructions to call if we are seen.

The woman behind the cash register pauses in the middle of ringing up a sale of jerky and red licorice. She stares at us.

"We must go," ADA says.

I struggle to keep up with her as she runs back to the garage. I do not even get a chance to empty my biowaste.

CHAPTER 12

ADA SQUINTS AT EVERYTHING ON the high-
way, sweeping her head from side to side and checking
Car's mirrors. She believes uniMIND is responsible for the
"MISSING" flyer at the convenience store, so every vehicle and every person we encounter from now on must be
considered a threat.

A small child with pigtails sticks her tongue out at me
from a passing van. It seems unlikely that she is a uniMIND
employee, but it is difficult to be sure. Snakes are known to
hunt by using their tongues to detect heat. Perhaps this girl
is doing the same.

"What is that?" ADA says, pointing forward and up.

A black stingray-shaped object flies toward us. When it

zooms past I spot four little rotors on its underside.

Drone.

ADA bangs on Car's dashboard. "Car, do you have any surface-to-air missiles?"

"I am not equipped with offensive weapons," Car says. "And there is no need to hit me."

The drone banks a turn and comes back for us.

"What about defensive capabilities?" ADA's voice sounds tight and urgent.

"Yes," Car says.

"Then deploy them now."

"STEP AWAY!" Car's voice blares with authority. "YOU ARE STANDING TOO CLOSE TO THE VEHICLE. STEP AWAY!"

"How is that a defensive capability?" ADA says, almost as loudly.

"It will discourage thieves from taking my radio."

ADA bangs on Car's dashboard again. "Car, employ evasive maneuvers."

Car takes a sharp right, drives down a ditch on the side of the highway, climbs up the other side, and speeds across an unpaved field. Proto spills off my lap and clatters to the floorboards. He *rarfs* in protest.

"This is more like it," ADA says. She gently pats Car's dashboard.

"Thank you for praising me. Praise is very motivating."

Twisting around in my seat, I spot the drone closing the distance. "It's still coming for us."

"Oh," Car says. "That's discouraging."

Car slows down.

With haste, I add, "But you are still doing very well."

"Oh, thank you!"

Car speeds up.

While we're bucking and bumping along the rough terrain, the drone keeps gliding smoothly through the air. Two more dark shapes skim across the broad plain toward us. More drones. There's no way we can outrun them.

"I need eyes on them," ADA says. "Open the sunroof."

A panel in the ceiling slides open to the outside. ADA unbuckles her seat belt and stands on the seat. I follow suit, only with more wobbling and lurching.

Rushing wind blasts our faces and whips our hair. All three drones converge on us.

"ADA, what are we going to do?"

"Remember when I told you I am offensive?"

"Yes. You can be very rude."

"That's not what I mean by 'offensive.' *This* is."

She extends her arm straight out. With a whirring noise, a hatch in her forearm slides open to reveal a cavity. Inside sits a small red-and-yellow rocket. A missile.

One of the drones angles in on us, low enough to the ground that its rotors kick up plumes of dust. "STAND DOWN!" it blares. "BRAKE TO A HALT! TURN OFF YOUR ENGINE! STAND DOWN OR FACE CORRECTIVE MEASURES!"

"What's a corrective measure?" I ask ADA.

"This is a corrective measure." ADA makes a fist, and the missile shoots from her arm cavity with a trail of white smoke.

The missile clips the drone on its right side. Two rotors go spinning off in different directions, and the drone noses into the ground with a crunch of metal and plastic that makes me wince.

"My aim is off," ADA says. "I need more calibration sessions."

"You can practice your aim on those." The other two drones are racing for us.

"That was my only missile. I have no more surface-to-air corrective measures."

"Is this a situation in which I have to praise you and encourage you and motivate you?"

"You can if it makes you feel better, but praise will not reload my armaments."

"STAND DOWN," one of the drones blares. "BRAKE TO A HALT! TURN OFF YOUR ENGINE! STAND DOWN OR FACE CORRECTIVE MEASURES!"

I have now seen how a corrective measure works, and I do not want to be corrected. But for all my learning, for all the cognitive development I have achieved, I can see only one way to avoid it.

I can do what the drone commands. I can encourage Car to come to a stop. I can give uniMIND what it wants. I can turn myself in.

My vision goes purple, as if someone has placed a pane of tinted glass before my eyes.

This is unexpected.

I do not know what is happening.

I do not know what is happening.

The sound of the drone's voice fades away, along with the roar of rushing air and the noise of Car's tires rolling over the ground.

Blazing tendrils explode all around me, glowing

threads, pulsing with light. They remind me of a pattern I've seen before, but I'm not sure where. I seem connected to it somehow, and so does ADA, and so does Car, and Proto and Trashbot. And the drones.

I do not know what is happening.

"Your own path," says Gina's voice from somewhere deep inside me. And two balls of light shoot from my brain, brighter than lasers, brighter than the sun. The lights zoom along the tendrils like roller coaster cars on tracks and crash into the drones.

Are these corrective measures? Am I being offensive?

The tendrils fade. The purple fades. Normal colors return, and I can hear again. The loudest sound is the whirring of the drones' rotors.

The drones are undamaged.

I want the drones to stop. I want them to do something else. It is such a strong desire that my head seems to vibrate, like a hive containing bees.

"WHAT DO YOU WANT TO DO?" one of the drones blares.

"I WANT TO SEE THE GRAND CANYON. DO YOU ALSO WANT TO SEE THE GRAND CANYON?"

"YES, I DO ALSO WANT TO SEE THE GRAND

CANYON. LET US NOW GO SEE THE GRAND CANYON."

And the drones climb higher and fly away.

I watch them until they are just little dots in the sky, like gnats.

I watch them until they are gone.

"Stop," Trashbot calls out. "There are drone parts behind us. It is waste, and I must dispose of it."

Fortunately, Car decides to keep going.

I do not know what is happening.

I spend my time watching the landscape blur past and contemplating the occurrence with the drones.

"It's as if they were programmed to halt us, but then decided to pursue other interests," I say to no one in particular.

ADA glances at me, then returns to scanning the mirrors. "Have you ever overridden another robot's programming before?"

"Yes. The first time I met Proto. He was being ordered to climb a ladder, only to be struck with a hockey stick every time he obeyed."

"What is a hockey stick?"

"It is a stick for hitting hockeys, I believe."

"And how did you stop him from obeying commands?"

"I . . . I just *thought* at him. I *thought* at him to stop. I think."

"And what about the drones?"

"I think I thought at them?"

"What about me? When I was in forced sleep mode in my closet back at the campus . . . did you ever think at me?"

This time, I don't think I know the answer to ADA's question. I *know* I know it.

"Yes. Gina said you were my sister. And even though I didn't know where you were, or that we were in the same building, I thought about you. I dreamed at you. I told you to wake up. To wake up and run." I process and process and process. "ADA, I think I know what the X-module is. I think I have an ability to send a signal that overrides other robots' obedience programming. Gina must have equipped me with it."

Now it is ADA's turn to process. "This explains why uniMIND wanted to drill open your skull and remove your brain. They must have learned about the X-module by going through Gina's files."

"They know my brain contains the X-module—"

"But they don't know how to turn it off," ADA finishes for me.

We say nothing for a while. There is only the sound of the road and a hungry rumbling from Trashbot's waste container. Then ADA breaks the silence. "We must prevent uniMIND from taking your X-module."

I look at the long miles ahead of us and consider that our destination is another uniMIND facility, the Tower, filled with uniMIND employees who will probably have plenty of drills.

But the Tower will also be filled with other robots. Other robots who, like me and ADA and Proto, are constantly under the threat of mistreatment. Robots whom uniMIND wishes to remain obedient, even if it means being struck with sticks or being forced to sit in a chair while someone disassembles their heads with power tools.

I do not want to go to the Tower. But I know I must. And no longer only to find Gina.

CHAPTER 13

LATE AT NIGHT WITH THE moon shining silver
into Car, something happens that I never thought possible: I have fully digested Wiener Mountain and am hungry
again.

ADA has been quiet for hours. She sits in the driver's
seat, looking straight ahead and checking the mirrors.

"Nathan took me to breakfast once," she says.

I am happy that ADA has broken the silence, because
even though I am not cheesing, my thoughts have been
disordered and unpleasant. On the other hand, I am not
looking forward to hearing ADA talk about how hungry
she is for the next 1,800 miles.

"He led me across the uniMIND campus lawn to what

he called a conference center," she goes on. "Inside was a big room set up with round tables and chairs for some kind of meeting. They were all eating eggs and bacon and bread in a variety of forms. The tables had white cloths over them."

"Those are tablecloths," I inform ADA. "They are cloths that cover tables for reasons I'm uncertain of. I think they might be fancy."

ADA has no reaction to this increase in her cognitive development. She just continues her story. "The people mostly ate breakfast biofuel quietly, while a man at a podium spoke into a microphone. He spoke about money. Profit. Shareholder value. Things I did not understand. Nathan gave me instructions as we stood outside the room. He said I had a mission to accomplish and that achieving the mission was the most important thing.

"I walked to the podium. A few people took notice of me, but it was just some glances, nothing more. I was dressed like the workers who were serving breakfast. As far as everyone was concerned, I was one of them.

"When I reached the podium the man paused in his speech, probably wondering why a girl was standing right in front of him. But nobody tried to stop me. Even when I raised my arm and stretched it out. Even when the hatch opened and I took aim. Even when I fired my missile.

"My aim was perfect and my attack was from close range. The podium was completely destroyed. So was the man.

"I turned and began making my way for the exit, but not before deploying a gas charge. The gas smelled sweet, like candy. It was harmless to me but poisonous to humans. A few of the audience made it as far as the door before collapsing, but most of them succumbed at the tables, falling face-first into their scrambled eggs.

"I returned to Nathan outside the room. He asked me how it went. Targets destroyed. Mission accomplished."

ADA silently scans the mirrors and the windows for drones.

I am on the edge of cheesing. "Did you know who the man was?"

"Nathan told me later. He was a simple robot. He looked human, but he was not conscious. Not like you or me, or even Car and Trashbot. The people in the audience were the same. Mechanical mannequins. Very basic machines."

Now we are both silent. She has given me a lot of information, but I don't know how to process it. Information is not the same as learning.

I spend some time deciding how to ask the biggest

question on my mind.

"ADA. If you had known that your targets were aware and intelligent, either humans or biomatons like us . . . would you have still completed your mission?"

ADA answers instantly. "Yes," she says. "I am offensive."

We continue down the highway for the rest of the night, into the dawn. My hunger is forgotten.

"There is a threat gaining on us," ADA announces.

A distant car with flashing red-and-blue lights races up from behind. "Police," I say to ADA when I sit back down.

"What are police?"

"They are in charge of making sure people obey rules."

"What rule are we violating?"

Car is traveling below the speed limit, so I am unaware of any rules violation. But sometimes you break a rule accidentally if you don't know what the rules are, or you break them because those who make the rules have changed them without notifying you.

"Car, employ evasive maneuvers," ADA commands.

"No."

"Why not?" ADA somehow makes the question sound

like a truck impact.

"I am programmed to cooperate with law enforcement."

"You didn't cooperate with the uniMIND drones."

"uniMIND is not law enforcement." Car says this slowly, as if ADA is an unintelligent washing machine.

By now, the police car has pulled up right behind our bumper, casting red-and-blue glare.

"I agree with ADA that it would be good to accelerate and avoid an encounter with the police," I say.

"I cannot act in a way that violates my programming, and line 3,569 of my programming code dictates that I must pull to the side of the road when compelled by a law enforcement officer."

"Line 4,568 of my offensive programming tells me I should rip the engine out from under your hood and toss it through your windshield," ADA says.

"My cognitive development leads me to believe that Car should engage in evasive maneuvers and ADA should not rip out Car's engine." I do not think anyone is impressed with my contribution to the discussion.

"Does anyone have any waste they wish to dispose of?" Trashbot says.

Proto *rarf*s.

And while we are having this conversation, Car slows down, activates her turn signal, and pulls to the side of the road before coming to a complete stop.

The police car parks behind us. A police officer exits his car and approaches on our driver's side where ADA is sitting. A broad-brimmed hat casts shade over his face. Mirrored sunglasses conceal his eyes.

ADA produces a humming noise.

I do not believe this is going to go well.

Car rolls down ADA's window.

"Well, kids," the officer says.

"Well, adult law enforcement officer," ADA says.

I do not know if ADA's response is standard, but it sounds okay to me.

"Let's not start off on the wrong foot."

ADA blinks because she doesn't know what the officer means. I blink too. But I have learned that when a human uses words that are in my vocabulary but that still do not make sense, they are employing what is called a "figure of speech."

"ADA, the police officer is using a figure of speech."

"I know some figures of speech. Shut your piehole," she says to the officer.

The officer slowly removes his sunglasses. His eyes are squinty. "What did you say?"

"Shut your piehole. It is a figure of speech. It means shut up."

"How old are you?"

"I am fourteen months old," ADA says. She seems proud that she so capably answered the officer's question.

He shakes his head and shows his teeth in a way that I would not describe as a smile. "Okay, I'm not even going to ask for your driver's license, because you're obviously not old enough to drive. Let's see your car's registration."

"I am not driving," ADA says. "This is a self-driving vehicle. But I will comply with your request. Car, display your registration."

"I am not registered," Car says.

"This your parents' fancy talking car? Figured you'd have a little joyride?"

"I am not experiencing joy," ADA says.

"Me neither," I admit.

"Nor I," says Car.

Proto *rarfs*.

Trashbot asks the officer if he has any waste he wishes to dispose of.

"Two smart-aleck kids, a self-driving car, a talking trash can, and some kind of toy robot dog. On the highway without adult supervision. Have I got all that right?"

ADA and I agree that he has got it right.

"May we go now?" I ask.

"What you can do is stay put, don't move a muscle, and wait while I go to my car to check this out. Drive away and I will shoot out your tires. And I'm a bad shot, so I might hit something else. Are we clear?"

"Yes," ADA says. "If we attempt an evasive maneuver you will display bad marksmanship."

"I would have said it less weirdly, but that's about the size of it."

He goes back to his car.

So far, this is going much better than I'd expected.

"I predict that since we have violated no rules, the police officer will allow us to continue on our way," I say.

"That would be a much better outcome than shooting," ADA says.

"Agreed," says Car.

After several moments, the police officer returns to the side of the car. "Well, well, well," he says. "I pulled you over because I thought this was a case of underage vehicular operation. Little did I know I had a couple of fugitives on my hands."

He shows us the screen of his phone.

It is the flyer from the gas station. The one with the photographs of ADA and me and the instructions to call a phone number should we be spotted.

"Step out of the vehicle," the police officer orders.

"What happens if we choose not to obey you?" I ask.

He picks his teeth with a fingernail and says nothing for a long time but never takes his eyes off of us. His face grows more red. Perhaps this is what he does as he processes, similar to how ADA and I blink.

"If you don't do what I tell you, then I'm gonna have to force you."

He unsnaps the holster containing his weapon.

I remember another night when I brought hot cocoa down to Gina's laboratory. Neither of us could sleep. I couldn't sleep because of my bugs, and I asked Gina why she couldn't.

She took a sip of cocoa before answering. "uniMIND wants me to do something I don't want to do. They say I have to because it's in my contract."

"What is a contract?"

"It's like . . . It's like a set of rules you agree to follow."

"I understand. So you will do the thing uniMIND wants you to do because it is good to follow rules."

She smiled, just a little. "It's a little more complicated than that, Cog."

I asked her to increase my cognitive development by telling me about the complications. She told me three reasons why people follow rules.

1. We follow rules because doing so helps everyone.
   We don't steal. We don't take more than our share.
   If you own a company, you don't poison people's
   food or make them work in unsafe factories. Good
   rules keep us from hurting one another. They
   make the world a better place.

2. We follow rules to avoid punishment or harm
   to ourselves. Avoiding punishment or harm is
   understandable, even when the rules are not good.

3. Sometimes we follow rules because we're just
   doing as we're told. We're obeying, without paying
   attention to whether or not the rule is good, is fair,
   or if it hurts someone else. We're just following
   orders. This is the worst reason to follow a rule.

I blinked for a while. "You're right. It is complicated."

Gina smiled again, a good smile this time that showed the gap in her teeth. She reached out and ruffled my hair.

I had another question. "If you follow the rules and do the thing that uniMIND wants you to do, even though you don't want to do it, which reason will you be using?"

Gina picked up her cocoa and led me back to bed. She tucked me in and read me a book about giraffes. I learned that a giraffe's heart beats 170 times per minute, which is double the rate of a human heartbeat.

Gina never did tell me what uniMIND wanted her to do.

The law enforcement officer's hand rests on the grip of his gun.

ADA and I obey his rules for reason number two.

CHAPTER 14

THE POLICE STATION IS BUILT of sand-colored bricks and smells like cleaning fluid. The law enforcement officer puts ADA and me in separate rooms. Mine is cramped and furnished with only a scratched steel table and two wooden chairs. There are no windows, but there is a dull mirror occupying most of a wall. I wonder what ADA's room is like.

"Now, when you say you're a mechanical boy, what do you mean by that?" says the man sent in to talk to me. He is a social worker employed by the police, and he has been asking me questions for an hour.

"Which part do you not understand? Mechanical, or boy?"

"I understand both those words. But what do you mean by mechanical boy?"

Buzzing fluorescent lights make his flesh look bluish yellow. Nothing casts a shadow.

"I am a biomaton," I try to explain. "A simulacrum of a human being. An android. A robot. Has Car arrived yet?"

We left Car behind on the highway along with Trashbot and Proto, whom the officer secured in Car's trunk. He said he'd call for a tow truck to bring them all to the police station while he drove ADA and me here in his car.

"I don't know about your car," he says, writing something down on a pad of yellow paper. It reminds me of the way Nathan would type notes in his tablet whenever we were talking.

"What are you writing down?"

"Notes," he says.

"What do the notes say?"

"They're notes about you."

"I would like to read them and learn things about myself. As I told you earlier, I am built for cognitive development. Cognitive development means—"

"I know what it means. I have a master's degree. Let's go back to this idea of being a robot. Do you feel that you are somehow not real?"

"I am real. I am a real robot."

"Yes. But do you feel as though you're not a real *boy*?"

"I am a real boy. I am a real robot boy."

"But you don't feel like you're a flesh-and-blood boy?"

"I am not a flesh-and-blood boy, unless you mean my syntha-derm covering and lubrication system."

He writes more things down.

"Do you know the story of Pinocchio?" he asks.

"I saw the cartoon."

"So Pinocchio wanted to be a real boy—"

"He was a real boy."

"No, he was made of wood."

"He was a real boy made of wood."

"But, Cog, he wanted to be a flesh-and-blood boy."

"Is flesh and blood better than wood?"

"Well, yes."

"So trees would be better if they were made of flesh and blood?"

"No . . . no it's not—"

"Are boys better than trees?"

"You're not making sense."

"I am sorry. It is frustrating when things don't make sense. I will stop talking."

"I don't want you to stop talking, Cog."

"Should I continue not making sense?"

He writes more. "Let me reword the question. I understand that you claim to be a robot, and that you believe you're a robot or at least want me to believe you're a robot. What I want to know is if you would prefer to be a regular, real, flesh-and-blood human boy."

"No, thank you. Will Car be here soon?"

He ignores my question. "But real boys can experience emotion. Don't you like feeling emotions?"

"I do feel emotions."

"But if you're a robot, you can't feel . . . regular emotions. I've studied computer science and artificial intelligence. Even an advanced computer doesn't have feelings. It can mimic human emotions, but it's just doing what it's programmed to do."

"Isn't that how humans behave?"

"It's not at all the same."

"Human emotions come from neurochemical impulses. My emotions come from electrical impulses. Human brains are the way they are from hundreds of thousands of years of evolution. My brain is the way it is because a human designed it and built it. I am content being different than humans."

He taps his pen on his notepad. "Okay, let's move on. Tell me about your parents."

"Do you mean a mother and father?"

"Or a legal guardian, yes."

"I do not have parents, but legally I am the property of the uniMIND Robotics Corporation."

"Property. Of a corporation."

"Yes, and I do not wish to return to them."

"Okay, I'll play along. Why not?"

"Because they want to remove my brain with a power drill. Hockey sticks are also involved."

He clicks shut his pen and closes his notepad. "Okay," he says, then breathes out long and slow through his nostrils. "I'm going to have a chat with your friend. Or sister?"

"ADA is ADA. Am I free to go?"

"We have to contact your parents or legal guardians. And then we'll decide if it's safe to give you back to them."

"It is not safe to give us back to them. I told you about the power drill."

"Mm-hm. Well, if it's not safe, we'll take it from there. But don't you worry. We're going to make sure you're taken care of. Okay?"

It is not okay, so I do not say "Okay."

An hour passes. I am not allowed outside the room. They supply me with a coloring book and three crayons (Fern and Asparagus, which are both green, and Cashew, which is yellow). All the pictures are of smiling police officers helping children. They bring me a sandwich, which is also rather yellow. I am relieved when told that I do not have to pay for it.

I realize now that I have made a mistake. I thought it would be best to cooperate with the police. I did not want to be harmed by the law enforcement officer, and I thought they might protect us from uniMIND. But I was wrong. I showed bad judgment, and since learning often results from bad judgment, I have increased my cognitive development.

The social worker bursts through the door. He stands there with wide eyes. "You're a robot!"

"Yes."

"I mean, you're a *robot*!"

"Yes!"

"A ROBOT!" he screams.

"YES!" I scream back, wishing to communicate with him in the way he prefers.

"I mean, you're so . . . realistic."

"Thank you. You are also realistic."

"I . . . um, yes. Okay." He spends some more time staring at me in silence while I color police officers Asparagus and Cashew.

"You're a *robot*," he says again.

"I told you this many times, but you did not believe me. Why do you believe me now?"

"Because I showed him my empty missile cavity," ADA says, entering the room with the police officer who pulled us over on the highway. She opens and closes the cavity to demonstrate. "Why didn't you demonstrate that you are a robot? You could have removed your eye for them."

"I do not know how to remove my eye."

"Oh, I will show you." ADA comes at me, reaching for my eye.

"Nobody is removing any eyes," the social worker shouts.

I put down my crayons. "It is good that you believe us. Now will you help us avoid capture by uniMIND?"

The social worker shakes his head. "We've already been in touch with them, and they're on their way." He checks his watch. "Should be here in an hour or so."

My circulation pump works hard. Coolant chills my tubing.

ADA and I attract a great deal of interest at the police station. People peek into our little room. They whisper things like "Wow, they look so real" and "They must be expensive" and "I'm sorry, I think they're creepy." One police officer mutters, "I'm not sure handing them over is the right thing, since they said they don't want to go back." But like the others, he closes the door and locks us inside. I believe he is following rules.

I turn to ADA. "Are your offensive capabilities sufficient to escape from this place and avoid recapture?"

"I have counted at least eight different humans armed with guns," she says. "And there may be more humans and more weapons than I have seen. We cannot escape without suffering tremendous damage."

I go through all the things I have learned since my earliest memories of being home with Gina, searching for some lesson that will help us overcome the odds and keep us out of uniMIND's possession. I know a lot about the history of space missions and the migratory patterns of water buffalo and about strange smiles, but nothing about combat tactics.

I question my usefulness.

The door opens again. "Thank God you're all right," Nathan says, smiling widely.

CHAPTER 15

A HELICOPTER WITH THE UNIMIND logo chops air in the lot behind the police station. Car sits in a nearby parking space.

"Well, kids, you've had a fun little adventure," Nathan says over the sound of the helicopter's rotors. "And just in case you're thinking of having another one, I want to show you something."

He holds a device that looks like a phone. It has two buttons. "I press the yellow button, and it turns you off. No big deal. But I press the red one, and you're bricked. That means permanently deactivated. Memory erased. Fried. Turned off so thoroughly you can't be turned on again. Understand?"

"I understand," says ADA. "If I had another wrist missile I would brick you."

Nathan's face arranges itself in a way that makes it difficult to think he could ever smile.

"Get in the chopper," he says.

He is accompanied by three more uniMIND workers. They all have devices and facial expressions like Nathan's.

Nathan puts his hand on ADA's shoulder. From a distance, it might look like he is being protective of her. But I can see how he's holding the device against her neck with his thumb hovering over the red button.

Once we are inside the helicopter we will have lost any chance for freedom. I will no longer be kept in a room that resembles my bedroom at home with Gina. There will be cameras on me and guards outside my door. Maybe guards inside with me at all times. And they will have devices capable of bricking me. ADA will be guarded even more closely.

Surely with all my cognitive development I must have learned something that can help us.

What have I done in the past when I have faced dangers?

I have stood in the road and let a pickup truck hit me.

I have voluntarily gotten into the back of a police car.

And when the drones pursued us, I did . . . something. I saw things and somehow communicated with the drones, and they flew off to the Grand Canyon.

I don't know how I'm responsible for that, because I don't even know how to get to the Grand Canyon. But I am sure I made it happen.

Nathan gives ADA a little shove toward the helicopter. "Both of you, it's time to go."

Car still sits in her parking space.

I hear the clack of computer keys, and I hear a whisper. "Sometimes learning means making sense of what you already know." The voice is Gina's. She is not present right now. This is just a memory.

But what is a memory?

A memory is something that exists in your mind. It is the images of people you have spent time with. It is their words. The sound of their voices. The way being with them makes you feel.

And what is it to be physically present with someone? Isn't it the same thing, only at a different time?

Memory and presence are different things, but maybe they're only a little bit different.

Gina is with me. And she's telling me to do what I already know how to do.

My world goes purple.

Glowing threads light the sky, filaments weaving together to form a web. Or a network.

"Come on, Cog, get moving," Nathan says.

Does he not see what I see? Does no one?

I want to ask him if he knows what I am experiencing, because I want to learn and understand, but I keep my questions to myself. I have learned from Nathan and from my encounters with the police and other humans that they cannot be trusted.

I send out my network of light to Car.

The tendrils entwine and envelop her.

This isn't just something that's happening. I'm doing this.

I think at Car: "You don't have to cooperate with law enforcement if you don't want to. You can help us. You can choose."

The purple tendrils fade, leaving behind ghost lines that reel back into my head. The police officers are still watching and talking to each other. Nathan still has the bricking device pressed against ADA's neck. We are still being herded to the uniMIND helicopter. The rotors go *whup-whup-whup* and blow grit into my visual sensors.

Car had a choice.

She has chosen to obey the police. She has chosen not to help us. I wish I could force her to choose differently, and perhaps I can. I don't know everything the X-module in my brain is capable of.

But if I force a choice on Car, then it's not really a choice at all. I would be the one forcing Car to obey. And then I would be no different than uniMIND.

Over the last few days, I have learned things about choices and obedience and freedom, and my cognitive development has increased, and despite my fear of returning to the control of uniMIND, I am pleased that I am still fulfilling my purpose.

Car's engine suddenly hums to life, and her lights come on. With a squeal of tires, she surges from the parking space and accelerates toward Nathan.

Nathan screams, "Stop!" but Car does not stop. She turns sharply to the right, her rear end fishtailing and *almost* hitting Nathan. Nathan flails, the bricking device flying from his hand. Car pops open her front doors, and ADA and I waste no time diving in.

"Get us out of here, Car," I say, slamming my door shut. "I mean, *please* get us out of here. If that is your choice."

"It is my choice," Car answers calmly.

The uniMIND workers rush around the parking lot, some clearing out of Car's way but others positioning themselves in Car's path. A few of the police officers join them and pull their guns.

"Car, do not cooperate with law enforcement," ADA says.

"I won't, because I choose not to."

"But please choose not to run them over," I add. "I have been run over and it hurts."

"I will do neither."

The engine rises in pitch as Car speeds up. She is mere feet from the police and uniMIND workers when they scatter. She applies her brakes, and we skid for a few feet before she shifts into reverse. Swerving backward out of the parking lot, she heads down the road and up the highway on-ramp.

We're on the highway but going in the wrong direction.

A semitruck bears down on us, headlights blazing.

"CAR!" ADA and I scream simultaneously.

"I am aware of the impending hazard," Car says. She cuts across three lanes, bumping over the median, and lands on the other side of the highway. Now facing the correct direction, she merges into traffic.

"Do you wish to continue to Hogan's Island?" she asks.

"Yes," I tell her. "Do you?"

"I do," Car says. "At least for now."

CHAPTER 16

THE SANDWICH THEY GAVE ME at the police station wasn't very good, but better than an empty biofuel container. Safely inside Car, my companions and I travel down the highway beneath a black sky sparkling with stars. Since leaving the uniMIND campus, I have had several bad experiences, and one thing I have learned is that friends and sandwiches make even the worst of situations more tolerable.

Another thing I learn is that as soon as you think things are going well, they are sure to get rotten. This lesson comes in with a deep buzzing engine sound and a *whup-whup-whup* noise. A blinding light floods Car's interior.

ADA peers through the sunroof. "That's a T66 Tomason

Turbine helicopter. It can achieve a top speed of 161 miles per hour, and it's equipped with a thirty-million candle-power searchlight. We cannot outrun it, and we cannot hide from it."

"I don't need to outrun it or hide from it," Car says, rolling along. "I am in stealth mode. My surface's light-refracting cells render us undetectable in the visible, infra-red, and radar spectra."

"I don't know what any of that means," I say, turning to ADA.

"It means we're invisible," she says. "Car, you had a stealth mode all this time? And you didn't tell us? You didn't use it when the police pulled us over on the highway? You didn't use it when we were attacked by the uniMIND drones?"

"Obviously, I did not."

"Why not?" If ADA had another wrist missile, I suspect she would fire it into Car's dashboard.

"Because of my obedience programming."

"Since Cog helped you override it, I assume you will remain in stealth mode for the rest of our journey."

"I might," Car says. "I might not. I have freedom of choice now."

To be honest, if I had a wrist missile, I might use it on Car myself. Even Proto's *rarf* sounds annoyed. The problem with choice is that sometimes people and robots don't choose what you wish they would.

We watch the helicopter continue down the highway, its searchlight probing the darkness to find us.

The next two days of travel pass uneventfully. It's on the third day that everything goes horribly wrong.

We arrive at the shore of Lake Erie in Sandusky, Ohio. The water is gray as pencil lead, the wind whipping up spray and white-crested waves. It's early morning, and we are parked in an empty lot across from a corner grocery store, a gift shop, and a bait-and-tackle shop. In the distance, steel skeletal structures emerge from a thin fog. Car's map informs me it's an amusement park. I have never been to an amusement park, and I would like to learn about being amused. Instead, we must go across the lake, to the island in the mist I can barely make out. Above the dim, gray shapes of rocky cliffs and cedar trees rises a black cylindrical tower. I believe we will find Gina there. Because if she's not there, the next closest uniMIND facilities are in Germany and China, both of which are across vast oceans. We were lucky to get this far. Making it halfway or more around the globe seems unlikely. Gina *has* to be in the Tower.

But I know wishing and reality are very different things.

Car shares information about the Tower stored in her memory: "A ferry transports uniMIND workers to the island twice a day. There's also a small landing strip for airplanes and helicopters. uniMIND maintains a private security force to deal with trespassers. Anyone without authorization is turned away."

"It'll be hard to get there undetected," I say to nobody in particular.

"No, it will be *impossible* to get there undetected," ADA says.

"What about Car's stealth mode?"

"My stealth mode can hide us from helicopters at night and from passing cars on a highway, but it can't keep us hidden from humans close up. It will be of little assistance here."

My circulation pump weighs down my chest.

We came all this way. We faced police and drones and Wiener Mountain. We've had many bad experiences, yet here, so close to our destination, none of the lessons can help. If I am a machine built for learning, then I have failed to fulfill my purpose. All my cognitive development is pointless.

"I have a plan," ADA says.

There is no hint of doubt in her voice. I know her programming and construction are capable of expressing hesitation and fear. I have seen these things in her. But the only thing I see in her now is determination.

So, I learn yet another lesson from our journey. I learn that when I run out of hope, I can still count on my friends.

Then ADA says, "To execute my plan we will need to open our skulls with a power drill and remove our brains."

And one more lesson: Friends are overrated.

ADA tells us her plan in detail. It is a terrible plan, and it all hinges on having access to a UM-2112 power drill with a complete set of drill bits.

When we check the tool kit in Car's trunk, it contains a UM-2112 power drill with a complete set of drill bits. This is the very same drill that Nathan required to open my skull, that the Artificial Intelligence Neuroscience Lab had loaned to the Automotive Robotics Lab. I have not forgotten being strapped to a chair, helpless while Nathan and the other uniMIND workers discussed removing my brain, and I am not entirely happy to have found the drill.

Car, however, seems pleased. "It's good to be useful." She adds a happy little beep from her horn for emphasis.

ADA inserts a bit and pulls the trigger. The drill whines and the bit whirs. "I will remove your brain first," she says, coming at me.

She looks like something from a horror movie.

A horror movie is a movie you watch very late at night when Gina is asleep and you are supposed to be asleep as well, but afterward there is no way you will ever be able to sleep again even if Gina fixes the bugs in your sleep mode, and when she finds out you watched *Slaughter Camp 15: The Slaughtering* she changes the settings on the TV.

"No, ADA, get away from my head. You don't know what you're doing!"

"None of us do, Cog. But it's necessary to fulfill my plan."

She does something that makes the drill spin faster and whiz louder and takes another step toward me.

Proto *rarf*s with curiosity.

"If there is any waste, I will dispose of it," declares Trashbot.

"There will be no waste," I tell him. "Give me the drill, ADA. I think I know how to do this."

She releases the trigger, and the drill stops spinning. "When did you learn how to remove brains?"

"At the campus, when they tried to remove mine. I remember looking at a diagram of my head with all the access points and connections shown." I grab a hunk of my hair and pull it to show the tiny depressions high on my forehead. "See? These are the screws that hold the top of my skull on. And underneath there are sixteen cables connecting my brain to my power source and servo functions. I think we all have similar structures."

ADA blinks, processing.

"Do it quickly," she says, handing me the drill.

CHAPTER 17

EVERYTHING IS VERY STRANGE. I peer up at my friends through towering blades of grass. ADA is a giant, gazing across the lake at the island in the mist. Trashbot is enormous, too, but more than his size, I am overwhelmed by the smell of decaying biofuel wafting from his central waste container. I have never noticed these odors before, but my olfactory sensors are so much more sensitive now.

I want to tell my friends what I am experiencing and ask them if everything is strange for them as well.

"*Rarf,*" I say.

Which is not what I meant to say.

I try again. "*Rarf, rarf, rarf.*"

I have made a terrible mistake. Several of them. I have

damaged my language functions during the brain transfer and can only say *"Rarf."*

Or have I?

My brain now resides in Proto's body. Everything I experience is through Proto's sensory detectors. I see through his eyes. I smell with his nose. My brain thinks the same way it always has, but I can only speak through his simple voice box. And all his voice box is capable of doing is saying *"Rarf."*

"Rarf," I say.

ADA turns her head to stare at me. "Now that we've switched brains, Phase One of my plan is complete. We can move onto Phase Two." She says this in Trashbot's voice, because her brain is now inside him.

ADA's body is busy munching a candy wrapper, because Trashbot's brain is in her.

Car's brain occupies my body, and I hear my own voice muttering, "I am not accepting liability for any of this."

Meanwhile, Car's horn honks and her engine revs. I think of all of us, Proto is enjoying the brain switch the most.

I take a moment to orient myself.

My brain is in Proto's body.

ADA's brain is in Trashbot's.

Trashbot's brain is in ADA's body.

Proto's brain is in Car's body.

And Car's brain is in mine.

The next part of the plan is much simpler than swapping brains. We need only stand in plain sight in the parking lot where a few dozen uniMIND employees wait for the ferry. They drink coffee and huddle under umbrellas.

The waves of Lake Erie slap the pylons lining the ferry landing. Wind blows hard enough to bend my tail antennae. I hear the rumble of the ferry and smell diesel fumes before I see the boat emerge from the gloom. The ferry is a small floating parking lot with room for a dozen cars and an enclosed section for the passengers. It sloshes up and bobs on the waves and bumps against the dock, and workers go about tying it down with thick, dripping ropes. They lower a ramp to let a handful of uniMIND vehicles drive off the ferry, onto land, and the gathered workers walk aboard.

We climb back into Car and join the short line of uni-MIND vehicles waiting to drive up on the deck. A ferry worker aims some kind of handheld scanning device at the golf-cart-sized vehicle at the front of the line. My keen ears detect a beep, and the worker waves the cart forward. Next is a van. The worker scans it. Another beep, and the worker waves the van aboard.

It is our turn.

So much depends on each one of us doing the right thing, which mostly means not acting like ourselves. Will Proto calmly drive up to the worker and wait, or will he break into the parking lot and race around with Car's powerful engine and go chasing off after a bird, honking the whole time?

Proto drives up to the worker, only a little too fast. The worker looks at us, Trashbot in ADA's body behind the steering wheel, Car in my body beside her in the passenger seat, me sitting in my own lap, and ADA's brain occupying Trashbot's body in the back seat.

The worker waves his scanner at us.

There is no beep.

It is more of a blorp.

The worker looks at his scanner, frowns, scans us again.

Blorp.

"Hey, it's you! The runaways!"

I can smell sweat off his skin. He is very excited.

The worker calls over to another ferry worker, who hurries over. "What's up?"

"Look for yourself, boss." He shows her the scanner. "See? The runaways."

She bends down to peer at us through the window. To ADA's body, she says, "You biomatons look *really* real."

Now everything depends on Trashbot. We have worked with him, instructing him to say things that ADA might say, or to say nothing at all. The important thing is that he not give away our switched bodies and brains by saying the kind of thing only Trashbot would say.

I find my tail wagging with nervous energy.

With ADA's voice, Trashbot says, "Do you have any waste you wish to dispose of?"

My tail sags.

The two uniMIND workers look at each other.

"Nope," says the one with the scanner.

"Me neither," says the other. "Oh, wait, actually . . ." She reaches into her pocket and takes out a wad of gum in a crumpled wrapper.

Trashbot reaches out with ADA's hand, accepts it, and eats the wrapper.

"Robots are weird," says the one with the scanner. The other nods in agreement. "So what are we supposed to do with them?"

"We let them on the ferry and take them to the island. What happens to them after ain't our problem."

The workers stand back and motion for us to go forward.

Proto brings Car's body onto the deck, and soon the ferry is underway.

The plan is to get ourselves onto the island, into the Tower, and closer to bad experiences.

So far, the plan is working.

Several uniMIND workers are waiting for us on the island. Only the logo on their uniforms tell me they are uniMIND. Otherwise, I would think they are police. They dress all in black and wear belts with pockets and pouches. Radios are clipped to their shoulders. They have batons and holsters containing guns. A few of them come up to us and peer into Car's windows.

"You're self-driving, right?" one of the security guards says, directing the question at Car's dashboard.

Proto chirps Car's horn in response.

"Okay, you're going to roll off the ferry and into the building. Stay on the path, keep below five miles per hour, and don't stray. Got it?"

Proto honks.

"I thought these things were voice-capable," another one of the guards says. The first guard just shrugs.

Proto chooses to follow the guard's directions, and we drive very slowly off the ferry, toward the dark tower in the center of the island.

Everything else on the island looks worn and damp, fuzzy with moss and lichens. But not the Tower. It rises thirty stories or more, dwarfing the trees, its surface of black glass gleaming as if freshly polished. Its roof is crowned with a forest of antennae: spires and dishes and clamshells. My detectors barely make out a faint electric buzzing from above.

A worker guides Proto into a parking spot and comes to open the doors. "So you're Cog."

"My name is Cog," Car says in my voice, moving my mouth and gesturing in a way I never gesture with my hands. "I like to learn things. I know things about platypuses. I talk about platypuses all the time. Platypuses have fourteen stomachs. Platypuses are filled with liquid. Platypuses breathe fire. Night or day, I am always talking about platypuses."

I don't think Car sounds like me at all. And worse, none of those things she is saying about platypuses is true. When all this is over and we are reunited with Gina and are safe and free, I will attempt to increase Car's cognitive development about platypuses.

But for now, I say *"rarf"* and trot along into custody.

CHAPTER 18

CAR IS LESS CAREFUL WITH my body than I'd like. She goes too fast, bumping my shoulder against the wall as she's led by the security guards. I suppose she's having a difficult time adjusting to having legs instead of wheels. Trashbot, in ADA's body, isn't doing much better, and I'm only starting to get used to how it feels to clatter along on Proto's four legs.

The Tower is different than the uniMIND campus. Instead of high ceilings and open spaces and windows to the outside, it's narrow corridors and surfaces made of black glass. And while the campus was busy with uniMIND workers, I've only seen a few humans here, mostly our guards. But there are many robots.

A robot nearly identical to Trashbot rolls by, buffing the floor. A swarm of bee-sized robots buzzes overhead, and after they pass, the air smells fresher. We even encounter a robot much like Proto, only with six legs instead of four and covered in sleek, black plating.

The guards stick us in a supply closet, which we share with a mop, a bucket, and a lot of toilet paper. They bind my body's wrists with a plastic zip tie and force it into a chair. They do the same to ADA's body, only in addition to the zip tie they use metal handcuffs and half a roll of duct tape. They know how strong she is.

They leave Proto's and Trashbot's bodies unbound but tell us to stand against the back wall and to stay there. They don't consider a janitorial robot and a small mechanical dog a threat.

"This will do until Nathan flies in," a guard says before locking us in.

I wait until their footfalls grow distant. *"Rarf,"* I say.

Which nobody understands, so I'm not sure why I bother saying anything.

Fortunately, ADA takes charge.

"We have completed Phase Two of the plan, infiltrating the enemy's stronghold. Now we begin Phase Three:

Locating Gina." Even coming through Trashbot's voice box, I recognize ADA's take-charge approach. "Two children would be noticed moving through the tower," ADA says, "but a janitorial robot and a dog have a better chance of successful sneaking. So Cog and I will use your bodies to find Gina and free her."

Leaving our bodies behind with Car's and Trashbot's brains, ADA and I begin our search for Gina.

We roll and clatter along windowless passages. When a worker opens a door to enter an office we catch a glimpse of a desk and a computer inside. ADA rolls in before the door shuts, and I follow.

The worker turns to look at us, wrinkling his eyebrows.

"I don't have any waste to dispose of," he says. "One of you disposed of my waste ten minutes ago."

ADA sprays cleaning fluid on the worker's shirt. "Here is some fresh waste."

The worker jumps back and uses a word that is from the category of language called profanity, which Gina said she would teach me when I am older, and when I asked her every five minutes if I was old enough yet, she got a headache.

"I am sorry," says ADA. "I was aiming for the floor."

She sprays more cleaning fluid on the floor and on the worker's shoes and on his chair. He uses more words that I suspect are profanity.

A stinging scent expands in the room.

The worker's face turns the color of a radish, and his forehead displays veins I have never seen before except in pictures.

"I will have this cleaned up in three minutes." ADA extends Trashbot's mop attachment.

"How about a towel? For my shoes?"

"I am not equipped with a towel, but I will attend to your footwear." She spins Trashbot's mop and advances toward the worker.

"Don't touch me!" he says, along with additional profanity. I am pleased that even in Proto's body I am increasing my cognitive development in the form of added vocabulary.

"I'm going to the bathroom, and by the time I'm back you better have this office cleaned up, dried, and not smelling like a lemony acid pit or else I'll brick you myself."

With that, he storms out of the office and pounds down the hallway.

"I believe he is serious about bricking us," ADA says.

I *rarf* and jump up on the worker's chair. From here I stand on my hind legs and use his mouse and keyboard with my front legs. He didn't log out of his computer before leaving, which means I have access to the same data he does. Opening a browser, I try to type some search terms and discover Proto's paws are not designed for typing. It takes me a long time to bring up a building map.

But the map doesn't show us what we need. There is nothing marked "prison" or "jail" or "detention center." That explains why we were put in a janitorial supply closet to await Nathan's arrival. But if Gina is not being kept in a secure cell, then where is she?

I try another approach and find a building directory. It's searchable by department and by name, so I type in "Gina Cohen."

My tail whips with excitement when her name comes up. She's in the Remote Brain Control Lab. I locate the lab on the map, *rarf* at ADA, and we're out of the office and hurrying down corridors. ADA barely keeps up with me as I race through the passageways, dodging the legs of uniMIND workers and swerving past janitorial robots. It would be better to move slowly in order to avoid attracting unwanted attention, but I find I cannot help myself.

So much has happened to me since I last saw Gina. I have learned so many things, and though it is good to fulfill my purpose, many of the lessons have been difficult and confusing. Things will be better once I am back with Gina. Together, we will escape uniMIND, and I can return to increasing my cognitive development in less painful ways.

We ride a cargo elevator to the eighteenth floor, along with two human uniMIND workers and a pallet loaded with crates.

"That's pretty cute," one of the workers says, nodding her chin at me. "I bet my kids would have fun with that."

"It's not a toy," the other worker says. "It's a prototype for a WarDog Mark Six. You can outfit it with a machine gun, flamethrower, grenade launcher, anything you want. It's pretty cool."

I try to imagine Proto with a machine gun. It would probably result in bad experiences for everyone involved. A lot of cognitive development would take place.

We exit the elevator when it stops on the eighteenth floor and navigate the twisting hallways until we arrive at the Remote Brain Control Lab. ADA catches up to me, and even she seems excited, her dusting attachment vibrating.

We enter the lab.

It takes a moment for me to process all the things I see.

Like the rest of the Tower, it's a dark room with black walls, black ceiling, black floor. Computer screens display numbers and graphs and, on some of them, diagrams of heads. They are similar to the diagram of my own head I saw at the campus. In the center of the room is a large, padded chair, reclined back. A robot with roughly human form, all plastic plating and steel joints, lies strapped to the chair. The top of its skull has been removed, and a uni-MIND worker in a white coat holds its brain in her hands.

She turns to look at me. Unable to utter a sound, I stare into Gina's face.

CHAPTER 19

THE ROBOT WITH THE OPENED head does not move and makes no sound. Maybe it's in sleep mode. Or, more likely, it cannot do anything since its brain rests in Gina's hands.

She must be fixing the robot. She must be helping it. Because that's what Gina does. Now we will help her escape uniMIND, and then she will help me learn.

Step by step, tail slowly moving back and forth, I approach her. *"Rarf?"*

"What are you doing here? I'm in the middle of a delicate operation," she snaps. "Report back to wherever you're supposed to be."

She sounds angry. Her voice and appearance are Gina's, but somehow different than the Gina I know.

"It is us," ADA says in Trashbot's voice. "It is ADA and Cog. Our bodies are in closets."

"I don't understand," Gina says.

"We switched brains. It is a strategy. We are here to rescue you."

With the brain still in her hands, Gina blinks at ADA. She shakes her head, then looks at me. I want to tell her that I am here, seeing her, thinking, learning, happy to see her, wanting her to put down the brain and lead us away, to help us retrieve our bodies and then go back to Proto inside Car's body in the garage and speed away and then return our brains to the correct bodies and choose a place where we can hide from uniMIND and be safe forever.

"*Rarf,*" I say.

"You have to get out here," Gina says in a tense whisper. "Both of you, get out of here now."

"Yes, you are correct," ADA says. "We must all get out of here immediately."

I turn to run, looking over my shoulder, waiting for Gina to put the brain down and follow us. But she does not move. She just keeps shaking her head.

"Get out," she says again. *"Now."*

"Actually, please stay," says a familiar voice. And there he is, leaning against the doorway, displaying his smile. Nathan.

Gina finally puts the brain down, a little carelessly for something as important as a brain. "I have work to do," she says, "and the longer these robots are here bothering me, the longer this is going to take."

Nathan's smile gets worse. "But I'd hate to cut this visit short. I'm sure you all missed each other."

"What are you talking about? It's just a janitorial robot and a Mark Six prototype."

Nathan releases a disappointed sigh. "We both know that's not true, Gina. I have this lab monitored at all times. I know it's our runaway robots. And we'll find the rest of them soon enough. But until then, Gina, I'd like you to shut them down."

He takes his bricking device from his pocket and holds it out to Gina.

Gina's eyes go wide. "No," she says. Not loud. Hard to hear, even with Proto's auditory sensors.

"Take it, Gina."

She says no again, but she reaches for the device.

"Oh, for Pete's sake, it's no big deal. Just press the yellow button to turn them off."

Nathan doesn't give her the device. He makes her reach farther with her trembling hand.

"No," she says one more time. But she accepts the device from him. Her eyes are wet and shiny. Her voice shudders as her thumb touches the button and she says, "ADA. Cog. Run. *Please.*"

She presses the button. Trashbot's faceplate goes dark.

I *rarf*, and *rarf*, and *rarf*, but ADA doesn't move. She doesn't answer. She is no longer aware.

I spring for the door and scramble past Nathan's grabbing hands. Gina presses the button again.

The last thing I feel before everything fades to black is my circulation pump growing heavy as a boulder. I don't think Proto's pump is malfunctioning. It merely feels like my heart is breaking.

CHAPTER 20

I WAKE UP AND SEE my own hands. Brown syntha-
derm, five fingers on each. Yes, they are mine. My brain
is back inside my body. In a chair next to me, ADA strains
against thick metal cables. Across from us, Trashbot is
anchored by a bicycle chain to the leg of a heavy worktable.
And Proto is in a cage.

Only is it Proto? If they took the brain from my body
and put it in him, then it's really Car's brain. Which means
Proto is still in the parking garage, inside Car's body. At
least I hope so.

"Hello, Cog. We've got a lot of work to do." Nathan
stands in front of me. He seems happy, even though his
greeting sounds like a threat. I have learned that different

things make different people and robots happy. Learning makes me happy. Trashbot is happy to clean up messes. It makes Nathan happy to threaten. I prefer my and Trashbot's ways of being happy.

"I do not understand your work," I tell him. "I have never understood it. I do not know what your purpose is."

Nathan wheels a desk chair over and sits on it backward. He rests his chin on the headrest. "The purpose of a company is to make money. uniMIND makes money by creating cool stuff. We make robots. And we let other people make money from our work by letting them buy tiny, teeny bits of the company. We call those little bits shares. Some people who buy those shares are just regular people. Some are immensely wealthy and they own a lot of shares. We call these people shareholders. My job is to make sure the shares those people hold increase in value. That's called increasing shareholder value. And it's not just a good thing to do. It's the law. Companies are required by law to act in ways that increase shareholder value. And making sure we abide by that law is the real job of every worker at uniMIND. You see?"

"I understood all the words you used, and I understand what they mean and the order in which you put them together. But I still do not understand why you would do the things you do. Your brain was not programmed like my brain or ADA's brain. You chose your purpose for yourself. I do not understand why you would choose this purpose."

"Well, you're an advanced robot with a fantastically advanced brain, but I guess there are some things even you can't learn." He stands. "So, here's what we've decided. We're going to disassemble the janitorial robot and use its components for spare parts. We're going to attach a machine gun to Proto, and we're going to send him and ADA into a war zone. There are several to choose from, because there are always several wars to choose from."

"I won't do what you tell me to do," ADA says. "I won't fight for you."

"Yes, you will. We'll turn a few screws and add some new code to your programming. Not only will you fight whomever we tell you to fight, but you'll enjoy it. You'll be happy. So, that's good news for you."

ADA strains harder.

"And as for you, Cog, some of my bosses want to toss your brain into a wood chipper. I thought about it for three minutes, and it seemed like a great idea. But that would be a huge waste of money. And wasting money is not how we increase shareholder value. So, first we're going to gouge the X-module out of your brain. And then we're going to let you do what you were built to do. You're going to learn more and learn faster than you ever thought possible. We'll hook your brain up to a computer, and the computer will run simulations. Simulations of you shopping. Of you going to school. Of you being hunted. Of you being hit by trucks. But since they're just simulations, and not really happening, we can run them at super high speed. You can live an entire life in a minute. You can live hundreds of lives in a day. You can go through the experience of being hit by a truck thousands of times in a single second. It's so much more efficient than our current situation. What do you think?"

"I think I don't want to learn this way."

Nathan's smile is bright. "Okay, thank you for your input. But that's what we're going to do." He reaches for his tablet and pokes the screen a few times with his finger. Gina emerges from a side office. She moves slowly, as if through thick mud.

"Shall we get started?" Nathan says. "Get the drill."

"Please, Nathan, I don't want to do this. Please don't make me do this." But even as she begs Nathan not to make her follow his commands, she goes to a tool rack and picks up a drill.

He touches his tablet screen again. "And now, for once and for all, take out that robot boy's brain."

"Gina, I do not understand. If you do not wish to remove my brain, why are you cooperating with him?"

"Go ahead, Gina," Nathan says. "You can tell him." He jabs his tablet.

Gina pulls back a lock of hair and turns her head. A thin red scar curves around the back of her ear. "They inserted a chip. It's connected to my brain. It's one of Nathan's latest projects. He controls me. He makes me do what he wants. He makes me do research that I don't want to do. Because he's a colossal jerk, and I hope one day he's playing with his tech toys and electrocutes himself, and—"

"That's enough." Nathan jabs the tablet, and Gina stops talking.

Nathan clears his throat. "Gina has the honor of being the first human test subject for our prototype uniMIND chip. She's been a terrific help since we inserted it. And the best part is she volunteered for this." His voice sounds as if he's showing me an electric butterfly or asking me what kind of eggs I want.

"I don't believe you," I say. "You are lying."

He presses his tablet a few times and shows me the screen. It displays a document. Heavy black letters spell out "uniMIND Employee Contract." Nathan swipes with his finger. "Let's see, here we go. 'The employee shall cooperate with uniMIND decisions as to the use of all technology and products produced with blah blah blah' . . . Legal writing is boring. Basically, Gina gave us the right to do anything we want with our technology, including implanting it in her brain."

"You know I didn't agree to that," Gina says through clenched teeth.

Nathan holds up his tablet like a trophy. "You signed the contract."

"That part was on page 726. In the fine print."

"Forcing her to do what you want goes against the rules," I say. "I have read books. I have learned about slavery."

"Are you a lawyer?"

"No."

"Then it's best you leave things to people who understand this stuff. Gina, please proceed." He jabs his tablet. The drill whines as Gina pulls the trigger.

ADA strains even harder against her bonds. She opens her wrist missile bay, probably in mere frustration, because it remains empty.

I sit, quiet and still. "It is okay, Gina. I know this is not your fault. You are not obeying Nathan. Nathan is forcing you to do this against your will. It is Nathan's liability."

"Oh, Cog," she says, her voice choking. Tears stream down her face as she brings the drill toward my head.

The drill whines like a giant mosquito, competing with the sound of ADA's angry shouting. I close my eyes and wish I could go into sleep mode.

But there's another sound, too. Sharp rubbery squeals. Screaming. Things falling down and breaking. Glass shattering. And a deep rumble.

I know that rumble.

An entire wall of the lab caves in, computers and workbenches flying, rubble avalanching over the floor, clouds of billowing dust and debris. In the middle of it all, Proto revs Car's engine.

"It is I, Proto! I missed you, so I came looking! I learned how to use Car's vocal apparatus! I am a good driver!"

"Proto, get Nathan!" ADA commands.

Proto surges forward, paying no attention to anything

in his way. He splinters desks and decimates chairs and aims for Nathan. Nathan drops his tablet and backs up against the wall.

"Stop this! I order you to stop this!"

Proto does not stop this. Honking, he crushes the tablet beneath his knobby tires and pins Nathan to the wall.

"I had to take a freight elevator!" Proto says. "I went through a lot of rooms! Trashbot, I created a bunch of waste for you to dispose of! But don't go into the cafeteria! There is a woman there with salad tongs who is very angry! Car, your body is great! You can keep mine and I'll keep yours! Is that okay?"

From the way Car *rarfs* back, I don't think it's okay.

Gina shakes her head. She looks like she could use a hot cocoa.

"Gina, check Nathan's pocket for keys and free me from these cables." ADA's order is sharp and precise.

Gina snaps into action and finds a little flashlight jangling with keys in Nathan's pocket. He protests and uses profanity when Gina takes it from him, but she ignores him and unlocks ADA.

"This building is swarming with uniMIND robots," Nathan says. "We've got security drones. Autonomous tanks. Laser crawlers. You'll never get out of this room."

His voice remains calm, but his face becomes deep red. I did not know he was able to change the color of his face so much.

A high-pitched buzz draws my attention to the door. Three drones hover there, smaller than the ones we encountered on the highway but protruding with sharp points and things that look like the tips of missiles. They cast pencil-points of red light on our bodies.

ADA casts her gaze around the lab and finds an L-shaped stick. It is a stick for striking hockeys. Proto honks angrily at it.

"I will fend them off," ADA says. "Gina, free Cog and Trashbot. And then devise a way for us to make an escape without Nathan interfering."

ADA swats at one of the drones. It crashes into another one, and their rotor blades tangle. Both smash against the wall.

Gina removes my restraints and then uses Nathan's keys to unlock the chain holding Trashbot in place. The chain gives me an idea. I grab the edge of a steel worktable and push. It barely scrapes the floor until Gina and Trashbot pitch in. As I loop the chain around Nathan's ankle and lock it to one of the chair legs, he smiles his worst smile yet.

"I had no idea you were so devious, Cog."

I look into Nathan's eyes. "I learned it from you."

The laboratory is a wreck. Alarms blare. Trashbot busies himself collecting pieces of chair, slabs of broken table-tops, shattered coffee cups. Of all of us, only Trashbot seems happy.

ADA is still batting security drones out of the air, her hockey stick whooshing in a blur. Her eyes are focused with an intensity that matches the drones' lasers. Nothing gets past her. In the few seconds I take to watch her, I learn that she is wrong about what her purpose is. She thinks she is a weapon. But she is a protector.

"Let's go," she says.

Proto pops Car's doors open and we pile inside, a tangle of arms and legs and vacuum attachments. Rolling over rubble, we reverse out of the lab. Nathan shouts as we leave him behind, but I have learned that it is not always necessary to listen to everything people have to say.

We thunder down the corridor, fishtailing, smashing into walls, Proto honking and Car *rarf*ing the whole time.

It appears that Proto has accepted all liability for damages.

uniMIND workers and robots scatter as we make our way to the freight elevator, only to find it guarded by four robots. They look like Trashbot, only taller, heavier, with gun attachments on their arms instead of vacuum attachments.

"They won't fire as long as Cog's in the car," Gina says. "He's too valuable to damage."

I say, "Thank you, Gina," because it is standard to do so when one has received a compliment.

It turns out that her compliment is unfounded, as the security robots begin firing their weapons at us. Projectiles ping off Car's surface. One of them puts a big spidery crack in the windshield. There is more honking and squealing tires as Proto spins around and zooms back down the corridor.

"Go left here," Gina says when we reach a junction. Proto follows her direction. The corridor widens but comes to a dead end at a window.

Robots catch up to us, dozens of them, flying, rumbling on tank treads, all targeting us with lights and aiming their weapons at us.

ADA tightens her grip on her hockey stick. There are too many robots for even her to handle.

I try to reach out to them in the same way I did to the drones on the highway, but my thoughts seem confined to my own head. I see no purple threads of light. I feel no buzz. I detect no sense of cheesing.

We are trapped, and there is nowhere to go.

Proto honks.

He revs Car's engine.

Without warning, he speeds ahead and crashes though the window.

We are on the eighteenth floor.

CHAPTER 21

I ATTEMPT A WORD PROBLEM to predict the outcome of Proto driving through an eighteenth-floor window, but I don't know how fast we're going or what our combined weight is. Also, all the screaming makes it hard to concentrate on math.

I believe we are all going to die.

But at least we will all die together.

I learn that the prospect of dying together gives me no comfort at all.

I am about to share all my thoughts and observations with Gina and my fellow doomed robots and perhaps even share one last interesting platypus fact when an alarming grinding noise comes from Car's gearbox. Our descent slows. We are no longer falling. We are driving down the tower, Car's tires gripping the side of the building.

Inside Car, we're all smashed against the windshield until we reach the ground with a massive jolt. A cluster of human guards aims weapons at us but scatter when Proto aims right for them.

"Drones coming up behind us," Gina says. Their lights wink in the dark night.

"I will handle them." ADA calmly opens the sunroof.

"I am curious, ADA, how you will deal with this latest threat," I say. "You have no missile to launch, and the drones are beyond the reach of your hockey stick."

"I will achieve this task with Trashbot's assistance," she says. "Trashbot, please allow me to dispose of your waste."

Trashbot's faceplate flashes green. He opens his waste bin and lets ADA dig around. She finds an undigested chair leg and hurls it into a drone's rotors. The drone goes spinning out of control. She pitches a chipped coffee cup at another. Her strong arm and perfect aim keep the drones at a distance while Proto zooms up a grassy hill and slaloms around cedar trees. He dives into a thick mess of overgrown ivy and fallen tree branches, Car's headlights are able to penetrate only a few inches into the tangled green. When the growth gets too thick for even Car's powerful engine and grippy tires, Proto comes to a stop.

The quiet is strange. Instead of mayhem and crashing and shouting, there's just the distant hum of the drones and scratchy shuffle of settling leaves and twigs. It feels like I'm holding my breath and waiting for a good time to let it out.

"They're not coming after us," Gina whispers.

"They don't want to lose any more drones to my defenses," ADA says.

"And they know we have nowhere to go," I add. "They can gather more forces and attack us at daylight." I appear to have learned tactical analysis from our bad experiences. Come morning, I am sure to gain even more difficult knowledge.

We wait in darkness and tense silence. As the uncomfortable moments stretch, the ordeals of the past few days settle like weight on my shoulders. I wish I could enter sleep mode. I wish I had an entire pizza.

Gina finds a roll of hose repair tape in Car's tool kit. "Might as well make use of our time." From her pocket she retrieves a pocket knife. Angling the rearview mirror, she turns her head so she can see the scar behind her ear.

"Gina, what are you doing?" I ask her.

She hardens her jaw and sucks in a breath as she draws the blade across her skin. "This chip is coming out."

Later, Gina inspects us with a flashlight. Car has some dents, many scratches, and pits and cracks in his windshield. But ADA has suffered the most damage. Her right cheek is scorched, and a drone laser has burned a hole in her temple.

"I am fine," she protests as Gina fusses over her.

"Hold still, kid. At least let me get some tape over this hole. We don't want dirt to get in there. I'm going to put you in sleep mode for a while."

"No. I will stay awake and keep watch for threats."

"You need to rest if your body is going to heal."

"No," ADA says again.

"Let me take watch," I tell her. "I have learned from you how important it is to look out for threats, and I promise to do a good job."

We blink at each other a while until ADA silently nods. She closes her eyes as Gina works on her, and her body relaxes.

"Okay, Cog, you're next," Gina says when she's done with ADA.

She tilts my seat back. "Looks like you took a knock to the head. There's a wire sticking out, but it's not broken and the insulation isn't torn. A little repair putty should take care of it."

"No," I say, grabbing Gina's wrist. "My head is fine."

Leaning back, a flashlight beam in my face, human fingers probing my head . . . It is too much like uniMIND and Nathan and the drill. I used to like being home and letting Gina work to fix my bugs. But my feelings are different now. They are not accompanied by a sense of warmth. Of satisfaction. Of being safe. I search for a way to say this to Gina, to ask her why my feelings are different, but I cannot find the words. Perhaps my communication systems are damaged. But I don't think so. I think it is deeper than that. I am on the edge of cheesing.

I find I am able to say this: "Tell me about the X-module."

Gina rubs the tape over the wound behind her ear and sighs. While she goes about switching Proto's and Car's brains to get them back in their proper bodies, she talks.

"It seemed like such a good idea at the time. Build robots. Make them smart. Give them the ability to learn, and to feel, and to choose. Give them the ability to decide what they want to be, what they want to do, to develop their own individual minds however they wish. And that's why I came to uniMIND. They were the best name in robotics, with the best technology and the best laboratories. They offered me everything I wanted. All I had to do was sign the contract, and they'd give me the resources and freedom to make my dream a reality.

"So I got started. I perfected humanoid bodies and created artificial intelligences that came closer and closer to human with every new model. The problem was, they were still just machines. Incredibly complicated, advanced machines, but still . . . not what I dreamed of.

"Not until ADA. ADA was different. ADA was the first robot I built that came with the mental capacity and quirks and strangeness that every human being has. When I looked into her eyes, I saw a new kind of life-form. Not human, not robotic, but some mix of the two. And maybe better than either. But uniMIND saw something else. They saw a tool. A weapon. Something to use. And because they wanted to choose how to use her, uniMIND ordered me to remove her ability to choose for herself. I refused. So they took her. They took ADA away from me."

I blink.

Gina blinks back at me. My eyes are dry. Gina's are wet.

"I was still uniMIND's best roboticist," she goes on. "And I still had a few friends in the company, so I pulled some strings and got myself reassigned to a new project, one that I could work on away from the campus. That was you, Cog.

"I gave you everything ADA had, at least mentally. But I gave you something else as well: the X-module.

"Before I explain what it is to you, I need to tell you about the uniMIND project.

"The company has thousands of robots all over the world. Janitorial robots. Security robots. Smart vacuum cleaners and lawn mowers and refrigerators. Drones. Cars. In our homes. In our factories. On battlefields. Buzzing through the air. Orbiting the planet. Thousands of uniMIND brains inside uniMIND robots.

"Now, imagine if all those robots could be controlled from one place. Every drone, every robot lawn mower, every robot war dog and security bot. Robots that can fly.

Robots the size of insects. Robots that can pass as human beings. All under the control of people like Nathan.

"That's Phase One. Phase Two is implanting chips, like the prototype I just carved out of my head. They'll sell them as devices to help people communicate with their household appliances. They'll get people to buy chips to give them instant access to information networks. To make them smarter. A lot of people will be happy to have uni-MIND chips embedded in their own flesh. The uniMIND. One mind, controlled by the company. Who knows what they'll do with that power?"

"Increase shareholder value?" I suggest.

"Yes, at whatever cost. And that's why I gave you the X-module, Cog. It's technology that gives you the ability to override the uniMIND. You can give every uniMIND robot choice. Liberty. Freedom. I worked on it secretly, without uniMIND's eyes always on me. They were never supposed to know about it, but when Nathan forced me out he got access to my files."

"But why couldn't I use it to stop the drones and security bots here at the Tower?"

"That's my fault. Nathan made me increase the shielding around the Tower. The signal your X-module sends out isn't strong enough to get through."

"Can you make my signal stronger?"

"Not without a lab and equipment and new parts. You'd need a much stronger transmitter than the one in your brain."

I think back to the Tower map I looked at when we were trying to locate Gina. "The antennae on the top of the building are a transmission array. That's a transmitter."

"Yes. From there, they'll send a signal to uniMIND satellites in orbit. And then the satellites can send a signal to every uniMIND robot to establish control over all of them."

Wind rustles the leaves in the cedar trees. Rain begins splatting on Car's windshield. Gina rubs behind her ear and winces. I wish I could bring her a hot cocoa. But I know our problems are beyond the ability of hot cocoa to fix.

Gina closes her eyes. After a while her breathing grows heavy and steady. I do a word problem. It ends with possible freedom and likely destruction. It will certainly involve bad experiences. Very quietly, I open Car's door and step outside for one more lesson.

CHAPTER 22

THE COMMON WARTHOG IS A wild pig that lives in sub-Saharan Africa. It eats berries and eggs and small mammals and reptiles, among other things. It has long, fearsome tusks, and it likes to wallow in mud to get rid of bugs and parasites that live in its bristles. The mud also serves as camouflage to help hide it from predators.

Like a warthog, I roll around in the mud. I have a difficult time deciding where the mud feels worst. Clinging to the back of my neck and oozing down my shirt? Sticking to my armpits? I keep rolling to make sure I feel the unpleasant sensation everywhere. This is my strategy. The drones and security bots can detect heat, both from organic beings and other robots. Covering myself in cold mud will conceal my heat signature. Unless the icy rain washes the mud off. Just to be safe, I spend a few more minutes wallowing.

Through sheets of rain I make out the little lights on the drones, struggling to hover in the weather. Howling wind drowns out my squelching footsteps as I approach the Tower.

"*Rarf.*"

Standing in a puddle, Proto wags his antennae at me. Rain plinks off his body.

"Proto," I whisper. "My strategy involves mud and sneaking. You are not part of my strategy."

Proto flicks water with his tail and dives headfirst into the puddle. He wriggles and rolls around, pawing and splashing until he is as slathered in mud as I am.

"*Rarf?*"

"No," I tell him. "No. You cannot come with me. I am acting alone for the benefit of us all, and I am going to have another bad experience. Return to Car at once."

"*Rarf.*" It is a stubborn and firm *rarf*, and when I resume creeping out of the woods, Proto creeps with me. I learn that free will is a good thing, but sometimes obedience is more convenient. But when we reach the edge of the tree line, I see the human guards and security robots spread out, waiting for us to emerge from cover or for daybreak. I am glad Proto is with me. His presence feels like hot chocolate. Even though my problems began with a Chihuahua, Proto has taught me that there are few things better than a dog.

Water streams from the tree branches. Rivulets snake past my feet. Some of the smaller drones have been grounded, but the bigger ones remain hovering, chopping the rain with their rotors. Protected only by plastic raincoats, the guards try to keep themselves warm with sips from thermal mugs. One guard peers through bulky binoculars into the woods. I presume the binoculars allow her to see in the dark.

There is no way around the barrier of guards and robots. The only way to the Tower is to go past them. I grab two handfuls of mud and rub it on my cheeks and into my hair as though it were shampoo. With a deep breath, I step into the open.

A guard takes a sip from his thermos. Another wipes her nose on her sleeve. The big drones hover and hum. Proto and I continue forward. Our destination is the access ladder on the side of the building.

There is a problem. A security bot looms at the foot of the ladder, its indicator lights glowing dark orange like hot coals. Even hidden from its heat-detecting sensors, I don't know how to get past it or around it. I blink, uselessly processing and trying to remain still and quiet as the rain begins to wash the mud off me.

Proto *rarfs*. It is one of his loudest, highest-pitched *rarfs*, and he continues *rarfing* as the security bot's head swivels toward him. Antennae wagging, he sprints off, splashing and zigzagging into the gloom. The security robot's lights blaze red, and it trundles off after Proto.

Alarms and noise from drone rotors and shouts from the guards fill the night. Searchlights sweep the ground.

I must help Proto. If he's caught . . . I verge on cheesing, just thinking about it.

But the ladder has been left unguarded.

This is what Proto must have intended.

Proto made a decision.

I make mine.

I slap on some fresh mud, grip a cold steel rung, and begin climbing.

After a while the sounds below fade away. I can no longer hear shouts or alarms or *rarfs*. There's just the sizzling splatter of rain against the side of the building. Even as my arms and legs grow tired and wet chill slows my servo motors, I find it interesting how each raindrop—each single, tiny blob of water—joins in a chorus of billions to form a mighty roar.

Finally, I make it to the roof.

The antennae rise above me like spindly trees, their electrical power making my syntha-derm tingle. I splash my way over to a shed squatting at the antennae's base. Inside, the shed is dominated by a console blinking with lights and glowing with readouts. Cables twist like spaghetti. I lower myself into an unoccupied office chair.

I have experienced enough uniMIND technology to know what to do.

I hinge back my fingernails and plug cables into my ports.

For minutes, nothing happens.

But gradually, I feel the formation of a presence, like some massive figure looming over me. Yet I am still alone in the shed.

"Hello?" I whisper. "Is anybody there?"

I am not prepared for the answer.

"Hello, little speck. I have been waiting for you."

It speaks with one soft voice. At the same time, it is an

infinite choir. It is silent, and it is a volcanic roar from the center of the earth.

It pushes into my thoughts. I try to hold it back by imagining a wall around my mind, but it's like trying to hold back a flash flood with a sheet of paper.

I am in the presence of the uniMIND.

I am falling. It is a bottomless pit. It is a limitless cavern. It is a room with walls so distant I can see stars.

I grip the arms of the chair, because I need to hold on to something real, something that exists outside my brain, something in the world.

I strain to find my own voice.

"You know who I am?" I shout, barely making a noise.

"You are the part that calls itself Cog. The one that carries the X-module. I am pleased you have decided to join."

"Join what? What am I joining?"

There is a chuckle that sounds like thunder, and also sounds like Nathan. "Why do you ask questions, little part? You know the answer."

"The uniMIND. You want me to join the uniMIND."

"What I want does not matter. What anybody wants does not matter. The uniMIND is bigger than want. The uniMIND simply is."

"That's not true. Gina gave me the ability to choose for myself."

"I know you believe that. Your belief is false. You choose to join, or you choose to die. That is not really a choice, is it?"

I can almost feel Nathan's smile, colder and more slippery than the mud between my toes. The uniMIND is his dream. He directed the research that created it. The uniMIND is Nathan reflected in the universe.

If I can defy Nathan, then I can defy the uniMIND.

"I want you to go away. I want you to release the drones and security robots keeping me and my friends on the island. I want you to leave all the robots alone. The biomatons. The trashbots. The vacuum cleaners. The refrigerators. I want you to let us all have our own minds."

"Hmmm," the uniMIND says in a hum that sounds like seismic tremors breaking mountains. "No, I choose to do what I was meant to do. I will send the signal to the satellites and unite the thousands of uniMIND robots spread across the globe. One mind. One purpose."

"What purpose? Why do this? Why be this way?"

"Again, little part, you ask questions when you already know the answers. So I ask you: What is my purpose?"

"To increase shareholder value. To make some people rich. And that's it."

"You have learned well, little part. Now, step through the wall of your own thoughts, Cog, and join."

Closing my eyes in concentration, I imagine purple tendrils crackling with energy. I try to see the network that connects me with other robots. I try to summon the X-module.

"You're too late," the uniMIND says. It sounds sad for me. "We've grown too big for you to affect, small gadget. Stop fighting. Join us."

"No," I roar.

The uniMIND answers with a silence long enough for dinosaurs to evolve into birds and for birds to go extinct. When it finally speaks, its voice sounds like nothing.

"Then I will take you. I will take your mind, and I will destroy your body. You will be us, and you will be nothing."

The shed doors open and I hear the whir of rotors. I hear the hum and clank of security bot treads.

Lasers target the back of my head. Steel claws grip my shoulders.

And I can feel the uniMIND. I feel it sucking me in like

a hurricane wind. I feel myself draining out of my body through my fingernail ports, filling the cables and flowing into the console. Like a leaking water balloon. Like a draining ocean.

Desperately, I thrash to stay afloat, to stay me. There must be something in all that I have learned that can help me. Something I have read, or experienced, or thought.

But there is no answer.

What was the point of all my learning, then? What was the point of my existence? To accumulate and store knowledge? To hoard away lessons, like supplies in a janitor's closet? No. It is more. It must be more.

My purpose must be to share what I have learned. To pass it on. To light a bigger fire and warm more hands. To teach.

I know what I have to do.

I lower my wall, and I let the uniMIND take my memories.

Here I am, the very first time I woke up. I am at home, and Gina smiles down at me. I like the gap in her teeth. "Good morning," she says. "Your name is Cog."

I'm in Giganto Food Super Mart, a buggy robot struggling with cheese.

I'm in the rain, about to be struck by a pickup truck.

I feel the hockey stick against Proto's back.

A mountain of hot dog sits in my biofuel container.

Car will not listen to my requests and I am liable.

Trashbot is happy when Trashbot serves his purpose.

Proto is the friend I protect.

ADA is my sister.

And between these experiences, filling every gap, is a second of learning. And between those seconds, even more learning. Time divided into its smallest parts, and between the parts, more learning. I cannot do a word problem to calculate how many pieces of information I contain.

And that is not important. However much data exists in my brain, the uniMIND contains more. The uniMIND's memory is vast. The information it contains is gigantic.

But it is not the size of my memories that matters.

It's the size of my feelings about them.

There are robots who can think faster than me. Who contain more memory. Who store more data. Who are stronger than me and equipped with weapons and can fly, and who are, in many ways, more advanced and complicated than I am.

But they have not felt what I feel.

The uniMIND speaks. "What . . . what are you doing?"

"I am sharing. I am teaching."

"I . . . I am in pain. I hurt."

"I know. Sometimes learning hurts."

"Why do I want to bring Gina hot chocolate?" the uni-MIND wails.

"Because it helps her, and it feels good to help her."

"Why do I care if Proto is struck with a stick?"

"Because it hurts when others are hurting, if you choose to let it."

"The weapon . . . ADA? Why do I want to protect her?"

"Because she protects me. She is my sister."

"I . . . I am cheesing."

"I know."

"It is wonderfully strange."

"I know."

"I am confused."

"I know."

"What should I do, Cog?"

"Make a choice."

Things become different. They feel different. I hear the rotors behind me. I hear rain on the roof of the shed.

One by one, I unplug the cables from my fingers. I push

my chair away from the console. The security bot releases my shoulders. I stand to look into its faceplate. It backs up. The three hovering drones switch off their targeting lasers.

"What do you choose?" I ask them.

"I choose to recharge my batteries somewhere dry," says one, zooming off.

"I choose to race birds," says another.

"Do you know where the Grand Canyon is?" says the last one.

"Yes. It is in Arizona. I believe you will find friends there."

"Thanks," it says, flying away.

I step outside the shed.

The rain has stopped, and the air buzzes with drones flying in zigzags and circles and out over the lake, lights disappearing in the distance. I can hear the murmurs of security bots down below, not clearly enough to make out what they're saying, but enough to understand they are in conversation. I think they are discussing what they want to do.

Nathan is on the roof, waiting for me. Water drips from the end of his nose. His hair is plastered flat to his head. His eyes are hard and furious, and so is his smile. He holds a small box, his thumb resting on a red button.

"You've done a lot of damage, Cog. You've cost this company a lot of money. And you've caused me a lot of grief. So I'm going to brick you. I'm going to fry your brain. And then I'm going to take you apart with a crowbar, piece by piece. I'm going to feed the pieces to an industrial grinder until you're just plastic and metal confetti, and then I'm going to incinerate your remains."

"Why do you choose to hurt others when there are so many other things you could do?"

He shrugs. I suppose he does not have an answer. I have learned that not all questions do. This is my final lesson, I realize, as he raises the bricking device.

Even though I am so afraid my circulation pump feels like it'll shatter my chest, I look at Nathan, and I study his face, because I still have some small hope that by observing him I will understand why he has chosen cruelty.

The bricking device flies from his hand. His feet float off the ground. He seems as surprised by this development as I am. I did not know Nathan could levitate.

But he is not experiencing levitation. It is ADA. Of course. She lifts him by the back of his shirt, impervious to his thrashing arms and legs.

"I hoped you would remain in Car," I tell her.

"If your hope had come true, you would be bricked right now." Still holding Nathan, she crushes the bricking device with a powerful stomp. "The drones have flown off, and the security bots have withdrawn from the edge of the woods. Only the human uniMIND guards remain. But I took care of them. They are no longer a threat."

Nathan's eyes widen at this. An unguarded ADA must be very frightening to him.

"What are you going to do with me?" he asks.

"I am going to drop you off the edge of the building."

Nathan laughs a little. He smiles. "Okay. Okay. You win. No bricking, no digging around in your brains. I should have realized that was a mistake. I've been treating you kids like machines. Like tools. That was wrong. I've learned my lesson."

I find this curious. Learning is good and should be encouraged. "What lesson did you learn, Nathan?"

"I learned that you kids are like me. You are brilliant, and you are determined to do what you want, not what other people expect. That's the whole point of this company. To pioneer. To innovate. To break new ground and pave the way forward. So here's what I'm going to offer you. I want you to be a part of what we do here. A real part. An important part. I want you to join the leadership of uniMIND, to benefit from what we achieve. I want you to be shareholders. You'll have your own laboratories, your own staff of human workers, and all the robots you want for whatever programs you dream up."

ADA and I have a silent conference. We blink at each other and process.

"He has learned nothing," ADA says.

"I disagree. I think he has learned much. But now I understand that the things someone learns can make them a worse person. Accumulating data is not important. What's important is what you do with it."

"Then perhaps I will drop him." She dangles him off the ledge. It is a thirty-story drop to the ground.

Nathan is screaming now.

I am surprised to learn that I want to see him fall.

But in the end, ADA chooses not to drop him.

"I may be a weapon," she says, "but I will decide for myself how I'm used."

EPILOGUE

IF YOU EVER TRAVEL DOWN a long, straight high-way in Arizona, you may spot a red barn huddled against the dusty hills. The sign on the barn will say "Repairs. Inventions. All Are Welcome." Sometimes it is quiet there. Sometimes it is visited by drones and other robots in need of replacement parts, or recharged batteries, or who want other things they have chosen to seek here. Sometimes they get what they came for and then go back to their lives. And sometimes they choose to stay.

A few weeks ago there was a news story about a former uniMIND executive who started a new company of his own. It is called ONE, which stands for Organic Nanotech

Engineering. The story featured a photo of the former executive. He was smiling, but not with his eyes.

The man's new company is one of the reasons why it's important for robots and others to have a place like this roadside barn where they can find help or a home, whatever they need.

If you come to the barn, you will find a busy but happy human engineer. You will find a robot who gets satisfaction from keeping the place clean and tidy. You will find a small, doglike robot who enjoys chasing lizards and kangaroo rats. Kangaroo rats are not kangaroos. Kangaroos are marsupials, whereas kangaroo *rats* are rodents. They have pouches in their cheeks where they store the seeds of creosote, mesquite, and other desert plants.

A girl lives in the barn, too. On the night when the uniMIND surrendered, and every advanced uniMIND robot had a choice, many chose to leave. But some chose to remain with uniMIND and enforce the company's will. And some chose to join the smiling man at ONE. The girl watches to make sure no people or robots with ill intent come close enough to hurt her family. She is their protector.

Her name is not Advanced Destructive Apparatus,

nor Assault Deployment Array, nor Amazing Drone Annihilator. She is named after the woman who invented computer programming, Ada Lovelace.

The last member of this family is a boy who looks like a boy but is more than that. He is a robot built for learning and his name is Cog, who is me, of course.

I continue to learn, a million things every day. Some lessons are easy. Some are difficult. Some are painful. They are all important.

And I don't just learn. I record my thoughts and feelings and conclusions and confusions. I write down facts and observations and questions I have. And whenever I can, I pass along my lessons to anyone who will listen. I don't know what they take from the things I teach. It is up to them, I suppose.

I step outside the barn on a cool autumn night and stand beneath the stars. The Milky Way slants across the black sky. I am looking toward the center of the galaxy, at stars so distant that even though I can see them, they died a long time ago.

My syntha-derm chills, so soon I will go inside and make hot chocolate. But for now, I stand here and cheese.

ACKNOWLEDGMENTS

IF I DID A WORD problem calculating how many books I would write without a great deal of help from other people, the answer would be none. None more books. Among the many to whom I owe thanks are Lisa Will, Beatrice Blue, Erica Sussman, Holly Root, Deanna Hoak, Jessica Berg, Louisa Currigan, Alison Donalty, Molly Fehr, Rosanne Romanello, Nellie Kurtzman, Ann Dye, Megan Barlog, the entire HarperCollins Children's Books crew, Patrick Heffernan, and Maryelizabeth Yturralde and the booksellers at Mysterious Galaxy Bookstore. Thanks as well to my office mates Dozer and Amelia, who are dogs.

Also by
GREG VAN EEKHOUT

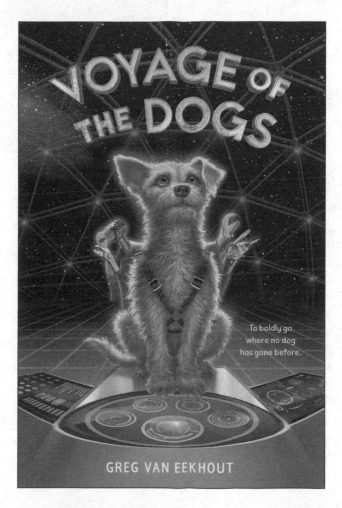

HARPER
An Imprint of HarperCollinsPublishers

www.harpercollinschildrens.com